# MORE BY THE AUTHOR

## THE REZTAP CHRONICLES

Book Zero: Mishaps and Mayhem

Book One: The Adventures of Reztap

Book Two: The Quest for the Insane Moth

## HORROR

Dissonance Junction

From the Shadows

The Dark Collective

Granny Bael

## ANTHOLOGIES

Unnerving: Volumes 1—3

The Mighty Pen

Tales of the Slug

# FROM THE SHADOWS

a collection of horror short stories

## LAUREN PATZER

**BLUE FORGE PRESS**
Port Orchard, Washington

From the Shadows: a collection of horror short stories
Copyright 2020, 2022
by Lauren Patzer

First eBook Edition November 2020
First Print Edition November 2020
Second Print Edition June 2022

ISBN 978-1-59092-869-1



For information about film, reprint or other subsidiary rights, contact: blueforgegroup@gmail.com



Blue Forge Press is the print division of the volunteer-run, federal   501(c)3 nonprofit company, Blue Legacy, founded in 1989 and dedicated to bringing light to the shadows and voice to the silence. We strive to empower storytellers across all walks of life with our four divisions: Blue Forge Press, Blue Forge Films, Blue Forge Gaming, and Blue Forge Records. Find out more at www.MyBlueLegacy.org

Blue Forge Press
7419 Ebbert Drive Southeast
Port Orchard, Washington 98367
blueforgepress@gmail.com
360-550-2071 ph.txt

*To all those strange and unusual.
I see you. I'm with you. I am you.
Be strong. We will persevere.*

# TABLE OF CONTENTS

# FROM THE SHADOWS

a collection of horror short stories

## LAUREN PATZER

# RAGE

As her pulse raced, Maria marveled at her heightened senses coming alive. She felt every heartbeat, knew every sinew as it stretched and elongated and could smell the fear and apprehension within miles. Her hand and feet transformed into claws before her eyes, hair sprouted from every pore and everything in her sight turned blood red before her mind relinquished control to what she had become.

The next hours were filled with glimpses of torn flesh, the sounds of screams and bones crunching between powerful jaws. She remembered the sensation of warm blood trickling down her chin. Guns and knives wielded by her victims were just as ineffectual as their bare, weak hands fending off the onslaught of claws and teeth.

She woke up alone in the forest, absent of clothing and feeling slightly bloated from the gluttony of flesh she had consumed. Most of the meat and blood had miraculously transformed immediately to energy, further fueling the evening's slaughter. She felt exhilarated, more alive than she'd ever felt before and couldn't wait for the next full moon.

That first experience followed the horrifying massacre of the small Romanian villages she visited a month earlier. It had been frightening and exciting all at once. She felt remorse for her victims that night, but considered them a necessary sacrifice on her path. She was determined that their sacrifice wouldn't be in vain.

The next few months, Maria intentionally put herself in harm's way. She positioned herself inside a violent gang's hideout the first time, working out the kinks of her biggest challenge—waking up naked covered in blood and gore. Elastic bands around her abdomen had proved too fragile and easily torn asunder during a single night's rampage. She'd resorted to piercings along her back that, while painful at first and somewhat annoying passing through airport security, gave her a place to clip the lightweight packs of wipes, paper thin garments, identification and funds.

By the time she'd traveled to West Africa to infiltrate a Boko Haram cell, she'd already gone through multiple transformations. Her victims had included a Klu Klux Klan organization in Georgia, a Russian mob group operating in Budapest and a dicey confrontation with the Yakuza in, of all places, Toronto.

Boko Haram proved to be the most challenging. It had taken months of research to get the Hausa dialect down, even though she knew getting it perfect wouldn't be expected from a Western world woman. She researched the Qur'an as well, but had to go to different sources to follow Boko Haram's exact vision and interpretation. Once she felt she had it down, the next hurdle was finding Boko Haram in Nigeria.

They didn't have a base of operations. Their nomadic movements proved difficult to predict, but she managed to find a few people sympathetic to Boko Haram. With a few well placed hints, she found herself abducted in the middle of the night. With only a week to go before her next transformation, she was thankful she hadn't needed to take other measures to find suitable victims.

She anticipated losing her carefully prepared clothing precautions, but they left her with everything. When they reached the encampment several hours later, she praised the soldiers once she found out they were, indeed, Boko Haram. They were surprised with her knowledge of their language and happily conversed. Once they reached the compound, however, the men grew silent and advised her to be as well. She was taken to a small building where several women slept. She was shown to a cot and advised they would speak with her in the morning. She was now a slave.

Conversations with the other women started shortly after sunrise. Many were retrieved to do the work of the slaves in the camp. When Maria went out with them, she was surprised when she saw thick woods around her. She was deep in the Sambisa forest as she suspected she would be. She just never really anticipated the woods would be so lush and green.

After half a day's work cleaning, cooking and otherwise seeing to the encampments needs, the leader of the camp summoned her. She politely answered his questions and professed her curiosity for their way of life. He visibly relaxed and explained their philosophy, adherence to the Qu'Ran and offered her a place among the wives of the group.

Maria smiled and nodded.

"But," she said, "death comes from the North. They come for the women. Did you not know?"

"The West thinks they have rights to inform our laws. We're well aware of the killers from the West," the leader said with a smug smile.

"I speak not of those Western demons, but of a blight coming down from the North. Have you not felt the encroaching cold? The wind brings an ill smell upon it and death follows closely behind."

Maria spoke of the cold, knowing a weather pattern was delivering cooler winds from the North. There was also a fire many miles distant in a landfill that may or may not reach the encampment, but she wasn't concerned about the literalness of her prophesies. She just wanted the women to be far away from the carnage she would unleash.

"You are trying to scare me!" the leader accused.

Knowing her place in things, Maria bowed her head to the ground in supplication.

"I only wished to advise you, to keep you safe. I offer myself to you as a wife. I would that no harm comes to you."

The leader walked around the tent for a few minutes, looking down at her form. She was as respectful as she could be at that moment and it must have impressed him on some level for he didn't have her killed.

"Very well, you shall have your wish. We shall wed tomorrow. Go get cleaned up and spend this final night with the women."

Maria got up, keeping her head bowed, and left the tent. She made her way immediately back to the women. She looked around at the dozen of them and wondered how many were there voluntarily and how many had been abducted. She thought briefly about asking them their stories, but didn't want to jeopardize the plan. It may be the only thing that kept these women alive.

That night, she stood by the door to the small hut they shared and stared up at the night sky. Just above the tree canopy, the nearly full moon rose slowly overhead. Maria felt a tingling in her skin. It wasn't time for the transformation yet, but it was close. Her own personal cycle of unyielding violence and bloodshed was about to begin anew.

She walked back into the hut and slid onto the cot, pulling the light covers up around her. She could hear the heartbeats and breathing of the women in the hut. She could smell their desperation. She could taste their blood seeping into the air through their skin. Suddenly, she sat up. Her senses were honing in on these few prey who would be the first if she couldn't somehow reset herself to focus on the men. She got up and stepped to the door again, peeking out. Her eyesight in the night was amazing and she could see the men all hundreds of yards away at the outskirts of the encampment. She picked them all out, one by one, and memorized their scents, their heartbeats and the flavors their blood spilled upon the night air. Finally, she felt some satisfaction and moved back to the cot. Even with her precautions, Maria spent a fitful night tossing and turning.

The next day, Maria went with the other women doing their daily slave labor, tending to the inhabitants of the camp cooking, cleaning and other various tasks. Maria noticed the men seemed to be keeping a much closer eye on her now. At first, she thought it was because the leader had told them they would be wed. But as the day grew closer to evening, Maria noted there had been no preparations for a ceremony, no additional food had been ordered cooked for a celebration and there were no whispers of a coming wedding. However, she did manage to catch a word or two of the evil eye and witch.

When she first heard the word witch, it almost made her stop what she was doing. However, given that would almost certainly give away her enhanced senses which would in turn encourage the thoughts that she was a witch, she continued on as if she'd heard nothing. Her mind raced as to how to counter this problem. Certainly beheading a suspected witch was not beyond the practices of the Boko Haram. She didn't suspect they would burn her at the stake or drown her like the old remedies of the Western world, but the thoughts she might be a witch was already a surprise. She didn't look forward to more.

Finally, as the evening arrived, she was

summoned into the leader's tent once more. She kept her head bowed, but she noticed she was not alone with the leader. There were several other men present.

"You haven't spoken of our wedding," the leader noted.

"It was not my place to say such things," Maria countered. "All things come through Allah. If He wishes our wedding to commence, He will make it so."

The leader grunted. The others let out breathes of suspicion. She could hear their heartbeats and none of them feared her, which was good. She decided to push the envelope nonetheless.

"I noticed the women are still here," Maria said. "You did not heed my warning."

"We suspect the danger is one of your making," the leader said. "You have been sent by Western powers to meddle in our affairs, disrupt our way of life."

This was not the direction she'd hoped the conversation would go.

"Did you not feel the cold coming from the North as I said?" Maria replied. "Do the Western powers have control of the weather?"

"You are wily like a jinn, Maria," the leader said. The others murmured their agreement.

"My apologies. I did not mean to offend. If the danger has not reached us by tomorrow night, I will gladly accept your judgment. I will die either way, as is Allah's will."

"Take her to the solitary tent. Two guards. Bind her, but do not harm her. It will be my pleasure to personally execute her tomorrow," the leader gave the instructions and she was taken roughly from the tent. As she was hustled away another man ran in from the Northern part of the camp. He entered the leader's tent.

"Shugaba," the man said. She could hear the man as if she was in the same room. His heartbeat fast as if he'd been on a long run. "There is a harsh smell from the north, smoke rises and clouds gather."

"Thank you, dan uwa na," the leader replied. "Take the women to the other side of the river. Stay there for three days. If you don't hear from me by then, assume the worst and flee."

Maria smiled and then quickly resumed a calm demeanor. She didn't want to alert her immediate captors that they were doing everything she wanted. Moments later, she was pushed down on a bed in a small tent near the edge of the encampment. Her feet and hands were bound. The taller of the two smiled.

"Go outside," the taller one said to the younger one.

"She is not to be harmed," the younger one said.

"I will not harm her. But it would be a shame to

waste this flesh that will be dead tomorrow."

The younger man shook his head and walked out of the tent. Through the flap, Maria could see the moon rising behind the trees. She felt the pull of the satellite tugging at her very core. She realized with horror she had misjudged the cycle in the confusion of the abduction. Tonight was the full moon. The women wouldn't be safe. No one would be.

As the taller man pushed her face down on the bed and flipped her robe up over her ass, Maria's heart beat faster, not with fear but with exhilaration. She felt her jaw begin to elongate as well as her arms and legs. Her attacker was inside her before he realized what was going on. He was a few strokes in when he abruptly pulled out and fell to the ground with a scream of alarm. His flaccid manhood flopped around as he tripped over the blankets suddenly tangled around his feet.

Maria's transformation was swift and she fell on the man in a flurry of fangs and claws. She ripped the soft flesh away from his exposed crotch first, eliciting more screaming from the rapist. His hands flailed upon her hairy back as her jaws tore through his vitals. In truth, he barely had time to struggle before he was silenced. She feasted on her prize.

The younger man poked his head into the tent.

"Keep it down or you'll be in a lot of trouble," the

younger man said. He wrinkled his nose at the smell of copper and sweat. He heard the growl of an animal guarding its meal. He ducked his head back out and ran for the center of the encampment, shouting "Lion! Abubakar has been killed by a lion!"

Then the rain began to fall.

From the edges of the encampment, dozens of men streamed toward the tent Maria was in. The rain streamed down and lightning flashed across the sky every few seconds. The tents around the camp emptied their contents of men in various states of dress, rifles at the ready. The leader ran to the front of the group, holding a flashlight and edged toward the tent. Water streamed from the top of the tent, splashing into puddles around the canvas corners. The leader pushed the tent flap aside, shining the light into the tent.

The blood and carnage that used to be Abubakar lay at the foot of the single bed in the tent. There didn't seem to be anything else moving inside. As the leader moved back from the tent, the beam of light fell upon Abubakar's severed head. He jumped back and fell to the ground.

"Aljanu!" he screamed and the first accompanying screams started to the right of him. He saw the flash of lightning illuminating a hairy beast slicing through two of his men and then disappearing in the darkness. The next flashes were from the guns of his brothers, missing the beast but tearing into some of their own.

Two of his fellows backed up to the tent. The first had his neck snapped by a giant maw of teeth and blood that ripped through the tent wall. The second turned and began firing, ripping the first man's torso nearly in half before a giant claw pulled his face half off his skull and a second claw went completely through the neck, propelling the man's severed head over the leader into the crowd of panicked men behind him.

The leader scrambled up to his feet amid the mayhem and ran to one of the vehicles parked nearby. He dropped to his belly and crawled through the mud, getting under the jeep. He watched in horror as the killer jumped and sliced through his men, although it was hard to tell if more damage was done by the errant gunfire or the devil beast he witnessed. Several times he raised his gun only to lose his target in the storm.

Finally, he looked out over the camp and saw no one moved. Something dug into his calves and he screamed as he was pulled from under the vehicle into the open. He scrambled onto his back and saw a giant creature covered in hair, mud and blood glistening in a flash of lightning. It towered over him and he pulled the trigger of his automatic weapon by reflex, striking the beast in the center of its mass driving it backward into the darkness of the forest.

He got up to his feet and looked around. The beast was nowhere to be seen. Still, he'd hit it with several bullets. He must've slain it. He struggled to his feet, limping along on his injured calves. He raised his head in triumph and shouted.

"Allahu Ak—" His cry of victory was cut off by the beast emerging in a flash and crushing his face within its massive jaws.

The women of the camp had not traveled far before the beast fell upon their party and slaughtered them with impunity. The three men with rifles were no match for the beast in the storm. After a brief flash of gunfire and twenty minutes of screams, the forest fell silent once again.

The next day, Maria awoke to a lion sniffing her in the middle of the encampment. The beast wrinkled its nose, flattened its ears and backed away from her. Around her in the loose circle of tents, beasts of prey and carrion eaters alike feasted on the remains of the Boko Haram populace. After washing at the well, Maria wandered the camp, searching through the various tents and boxes of belongings until she found enough clothing to assemble an outfit. She looked south toward the last remnants of the encampment, who would now be decomposing amongst the forest undergrowth. She bowed her head and tears fell freely. The innocent and the guilty both fell victim to her curse last night. She was damned again.

# THE PATCHWORK MAN

I just wanted to thank you," Barron said as he tightened the straps holding the young man to the custom steel table.

"For what?" the young blonde haired man said. "Does that mean you're going to let me go?"

"No," Barton said as he pulled a piece of tape and pressed it firmly across the young man's mouth. "I wanted to thank you for being young and healthy. It will add so many years to my life."

Barton brushed the hair out of the frightened young man's face. "You're really near the end of my experiment. Sixty people have given their life essence to extend my life span, including the one who let slip the secret of eternal life. Although, I must confess, his ramblings about limitations never ceased to make me wonder."

Barton removed his gloves and the young man's

eyes widened with surprise. Barton's hand resembled a quilt. No less than four patches of skin, all different colors and stitched together with scars, made up the surface of his right hand. The young man's eyes traveled to Barton's face and exposed skin at his throat. There, barely visible in the shadows, were more scars amid different colored patches of skin.

"The process is a bit painful at first, as peeling a bit of skin back normally is. If it makes you feel any better, I experience the same pain when I prepare my own flesh for the procedure. Unfortunately, drugs interfere with the process so there will be no anesthesia."

Barton double wrapped the young man's left wrist to the thick steel shelf underneath, ensuring the arm that was already secured would not move. Barton pulled at the fingers of the young man's left hand, but he resisted, curving the fingers down into a fist.

Barton reached to the center of victim's shirt and ripped the garment open.

"I don't require any flesh from the rest of your body, so if you don't cooperate, the pain will increase exponentially," Barton said and reached to a tool bench behind him. He retrieved a red hot iron and held it over the young man's face.

"Do you feel the heat?"

The young man nodded his head.

"Shall I apply the iron to your abdomen so you can feel the pain?"

The young man shook his head vigorously.

Barton moved the iron over the young man's flesh and he watched the young man's eyes go wide as he felt the wave of heat coming from the red hot surface inches away from his skin.

"Don't make this more difficult than it has to be," Barton said and moved the iron back to the work bench. He quickly set to work taping each down finger down to the individual curved steel bars set into the end of the shelf. He set his eyes on the young man's head and pulled out a length of the duct tape and wrapped it around the man's forehead, securing his head to the table so it was barely movable.

"The process requires delicate precision, hard to accomplish with you thrashing about. Hence, you've been most expertly secured to this custom, heavily weighted table. The only comfort I can offer you is that the ceremony and procedure will be over in a matter of minutes and then you'll no longer be in pain because you'll be dead," Barton smiled thinly as he finished the last.

Finally, he turned back to the work bench and retrieved the scalpel. He examined the back of his own hand for a moment, mentally measuring the single piece of original skin that still remained there, taking in the size and shape of the flesh. He then set to the task of cutting into the back of the young man's hand, ignoring the muffled screams of pain as the blade bit into the flesh. Blood streamed from the fresh incision as Barton expertly carved the skin into a single flap, lifting it up from the flesh beneath leaving a small amount of skin still connected.

Barton then proceeded to cut into the back of his own hand, following the same procedure, wincing as he carved his own flesh away, leaving a flap on the opposite side as that of the young man's. His own blood hit the plastic covered floor, his own surgical booties and gown, mixing indistinguishably with the young man's blood already present. When the cut was complete, he set the blade on the table next to the young man and retrieved the sutures and thread just next to him on a small rolling table.

Barton moved his left hand into place under the young man's flap of skin. As he did so, he began to chant an ancient text known only to a select few. As the stitches secured the young man's skin to his own hand, the young man screamed an altogether different kind of muffled sound as his flesh noticeably aged with each stitch completed and each word that was spoken. At the end of a grueling ten minutes of stitches and chanting, it was complete.

Barton cut the last bit of skin from the young man whose body was now an aged and desiccated corpse. After he sliced the remaining last bit of his own flesh, he stitched the last part of the young man's flesh into his patchwork left hand. He held the hand up to the light and nodded. He moved to the sink and washed the blood away from his stitched hand. He closed his eyes and could feel the invigorating life force flowing through him from his latest victim. The rush was something he would miss.

"So now I'm in you?" the young man's unmistakable voice said behind Barton. Barton whirled around to see the young man sitting in perfect health on the table with the exception of the bit of flesh missing from his left hand, dripping blood onto the floor with a dull splash. "Interesting."

Barton glanced at his hand again and confirmed the flesh from the man was now attached to his body. Even now, the dark edges of the incision were fading and healing into the tell tale scars he had over the majority of his body. He glanced at the man on the table who cocked his head curiously at him. Keeping the man in sight, Barton edged around the room and opened the door. He exited the door and flipped the padlock into place, securing it from any casual intrusions. He turned around, expecting to be in the hallway of his mansion, but instead, he was simply in another room similar to the one he'd just left. The furnishings were older dating to approximately the 1870s. It took a moment for him to realize he was now in the room where he'd dispatched his mentor and taken on a slice of his flesh.

"Curious what happens when you're given a gift and you get greedy?" another man's voice asked him. It was a voice he hadn't heard in more than a century, a voice that matched the Victorian furniture in the room.

"McCreedy?" Barton gasped. "That's impossible! You've been dead for a hundred and fifty years!"

"I warned you, but you didn't listen. Then you made the critical mistake. You made me one of your victims!" The voice echoed throughout the small room. Desperate for an answer to the source, Barton raced to the cupboards and threw them open. There had to be a speaker, or a megaphone hidden somewhere.

"I'll find you and end you!" Barton screamed as he pulled everything from the cupboards, old style pottery, glasses and jugs crashing to the ground behind him. As soon as he'd emptied everything, he leaned back against the table in the center of the room. Everything had been flung open, emptied on the floor of the damp and musty room. The cupboards, laid bare, revealed nothing.

"You've made quite a mess of things," McCreedy said from behind Barton. Startled, he spun on his heels and backed into the cupboards. There, on the rough wooden table adorned with cutouts for arms and legs lay his old mentor, Albert McCreedy. With no clothing but a small breechcloth to cover him, he was a tapestry of colors and shades, hair of different colors sprouting from the patched together bits of skin on his legs, arms and torso. His face alone was unblemished. He stared up into the single lamplight hanging overhead, mouth agape as he had been the night Barton had taken his life.

Then he sat up and leaned on one elbow, with a big smile on his face.

"How can you end me when I'm part of you now?" McCreedy said and erupted with a dark maniacal laugh that shook Barton to his bones.

"I don't believe it. It's a hallucination," Barton said calmly. He closed his eyes and took a deep breath. He opened them again and McCreedy was gone, but the room he had killed his benefactor in remained, kitchenware strewn about the floor. Barton looked left and right. Unlike the room so many years ago, there were three doors to the room including the one he'd entered through just across from him. In history, there had been but a single entrance. It was an aptly named dead end. Barton took the door to the left.

He boldly walked through the door, fully anticipating he'd be in the hallway of his mansion. But there, in front of him, was another blast from the past. The room he'd used in Bulgaria in the 1920's was arrayed before him. A large stone walled room in the basement of an opulent estate. In the center of the room lay a stone slab with wooden dowels arranged around it at regular intervals; the perfect design to immobilize a living victim before peeling off a strip of their flesh.

Barton turned to leave immediately; this room he couldn't stand. He couldn't tolerate the memories. The door he'd walked through had disappeared. He looked to the right where the staircase to the upper floors had been located a century ago. The staircase was gone. He looked around wildly, his mind racing for some way, any way to escape the room.

"No," he whispered to the room. "I can't…"

"Oh, but you did," came the sultry reply from the behind him.

"Anna," Barton whispered, his voice barely audible. He fixed his gaze on the stone floor stained with dried and fresh blood. It appeared just like the last time he'd seen it.

"I'm amazed you remember my name," she replied.

"I could never forget you," Barton said, louder

but still strained. His gaze rose and he saw her standing on the table, blood dripping from her right bicep where a rectangle of flesh announced its absence with a fiery red canvas of bubbling muscle tissue. The angry wound pulsed and throbbed like a thing alive all unto its own. Barton watched as it pulsed in time with his own heartbeat, drops of blood oozing from the lower part of the incision, adding to the increasing flow of crimson leaving a trail down her arm and leg.

She leapt from the table over the dowels and landed on the floor in front of him, a stream of red fury trailing behind her in the air. It hung in the air like a winged serpent, winding its way around the room.

"You could have left me alive while you fled like a coward unable to face your crimes!" Anna shouted.

"You should have left it alone!" Barton cried out. "Why couldn't you have just left it alone? I loved you."

"How can a killer like you love anything but yourself?" Anna shouted again. "Too long have I been silent. I will haunt you for all eternity."

Anna stepped forward and pointed her finger at Barton. The crimson dragon floating through the air darted toward him and coalesced around his throat. Barton grasped at the serpent, but his hands went through the hot blood and he could grasp nothing of substance. It flowed into his mouth and his nostrils and he felt himself drowning as the hot liquid filled his lungs. He fell to the ground, his chest burning. His hands clawed at the ground as his eyes focused on his hands, the patchwork there glowing with each pulse of his heart as he struggled to stay alive.

The floor fell out beneath him and Barton hit the ground hard. The last bit of air was forced out of his lungs along with a fountain of blood as he collided with the grassy surface below him. He rolled onto his back and gasped for air. The suffocating serpent had evaporated into thin air.

At last, he was outside. Whatever madness had taken him seemed to be gone for now. He sat up and his blood turned to ice. He immediately recognized the woods on either side of him led to a small glen just thirty yards ahead. Barton got to his feet and stumbled forward; dreading what was to come but knowing for certainty that he deserved whatever punishment might come forth.

"You remember this, of course," McCreedy said. Barton looked to the right and saw the other patchwork man walking beside him, dressed in the same manner he had been that day. The older man wore a plain tunic and breechcloth pants along with some worn sandals. Things easily thrown in a fire and burned to hide the crime they would hold the evidence for.

"Never again," Barton muttered.

McCreedy shrugged. "To get the most efficient use of a lifetime, you have to start as early as possible. It's really just simple math."

Barton grasped his side as a burning pain reminded him of the first patch of skin he'd grafted onto himself.

"You never told me this would happen," Barton said between gritted teeth.

"I told you the rules and you chose to ignore them," McCreedy said. "You didn't just absorb the life force, my greedy apprentice. You absorbed the souls. There's only so much room inside you for that kind of power. Only so much you can suppress naturally. Of course, there was also the added soul bonanza you hadn't really counted on."

"What are you talking about?"

"I know what's going through your mind. Just rip off the last patch of skin and take your total back to sixty," McCreedy said. Barton clenched his jaw. The thought had crossed his mind. Drop back to sixty patches, take whatever damage might occur and move forward, wounded but wiser.

"I suppose you're going to tell me that won't work," Barton said. With each step closer to the glen, the weight of his feet increased dramatically. The burning in his side grew more intense the closer they got.

"I held them back," McCreedy said. "How many did I take with me before you absorbed my life essence?"

Barton stopped walking and slowly looked over at the old man.

"Oh, now the math kicks in!" McCreedy cackled. "You're at well over a hundred, old friend! You got my years as well as everything else! Each life will rip apart at your soul until you pass the final threshold, which should be several thousand years now. Your desiccated body rotting away in a hole under your mansion, unable to move and unable to die, suffering for centuries for the lives you've taken!"

McCreedy howled with laughter. Barton scrunched up his face, turned back to the glen and plodded forward.

There on a stone table in the middle of the glen lay a young boy, a wound on his side matching the one where Barton had taken a patch of flesh from him so long ago. This wound didn't bleed, though. Fire rose from the wound like the fuel from a hearth was contained within. The boy sat up and turned to look at Barton. The fire in his pupils seemed to burn a hole right through Barton's soul.

Flames burst forth from Barton's side. He fell to the ground screaming in agony. Fire consumed him and he felt the skin melting off his flesh. His muscular tissue bubbled with heat as it cooked. His bones turned to ash and he rose up into the sky as smoke and pain until he coalesced once more into a solid form again back within his master's chamber.

Barton lay on the floor for a long time. He stared at the ceiling of the room, the old timbers there bearing witness to the slaughter of so many on the table at his side. Had McCreedy killed all forty victims in this room or had he traveled extensively, covering his tracks in each town as Barton had?

"You may think you can lie there forever, but that's not how it works," McCreedy said, his feet dangling off the table, swinging back and forth.

Barton sat up and looked at the door he'd passed through before and seen Anna. Anything but that was bearable. If he could make it through eternity without ever facing her wrath again, he could survive.

Barton got up and moved to the other door.

"What's entertaining is you think you have a choice in your punishment, but now it's all your victims in control. If you don't move through a portal, they'll drag you kicking and screaming. They choose who will torment your soul next."

Barton looked back at McCreedy, his soul full of hate and loathing.

McCreedy smiled at him. "Your bitter hatred only makes me feel better."

Barton turned away, opened the door in front of him and stepped through.

Jenna pulled her brother from the rideshare sedan. He shook his head.

"This is a really horrible idea," Jake said as he tugged at the tight leather pants she'd convinced him to wear. She brushed his blonde hair aside and pinched his cheek.

"Three months is too long to sulk," Jenna said. She grabbed his hand and pulled him up the long walk to the faintly lit mansion. Lights sparkled through the windows and music pounded out into the warm, night air with a rhythmic beat that Jake had to admit was catchy.

"I can just be single, you know," Jake said. His sister laughed hard and he frowned.

"You are not good by yourself," Jenna said. "You're pale, you've lost weight and thank goodness I finally convinced you to take a shower. Mom was getting pissed."

"Sure, poke fun at my misery," Jake said. In his mind, he saw his ex-girlfriend Bella walking out the door. "I'm still not ready."

"You don't know that until you try," Jenna said. He looked at her in the mansion's porch light. Her body was barely covered by the tight skirt and midriff shirt. It hugged every curve leaving very little to the imagination.

"You're sure not afraid," Jake said.

Jenna flicked her blonde hair and smiled. She opened the door and light flooded out. Jake noticed she had worn the powder with the glitter in it. Jenna pulled him inside.

The music was just short of too loud for the enclosed mansion. Looking around, Jake noticed everyone seemed on the young side, same age range as him and his twin. Ubiquitous red cups dotted the room as the party attendants drank, danced and generally hung on each other in very comfortable, heated ways. Jenna tugged him through the crowd into the kitchen area where they found their own drinks being served by a middle aged, dark-haired man in a tuxedo.

"Greetings, I'm Darryx, your host for the evening. What can I get you to drink?" Darryx said, giving them a warm, genuine smile.

"Anything with tequila in it," Jenna said. "Thanks!"

"Of course," Darryx replied. It was at this moment he gave Jenna the once over. Jake noticed the man's eyes lingering a bit too long on his sister's body before the older man made her drink. Jenna's attention was elsewhere, so she didn't notice the blatant leer coming from their host. Darryx made the drink and tapped Jenna on the shoulder. She thanked him again and walked into the crowd.

"And for you?" Darryx asked.

"Just a soda, thanks. Cola would be fine," Jake replied. The man then gave Jake the same appraising once over and Jake immediately felt creeped out. Darryx turned his attention to Jake's drink and finished it up in short order, handing it to Jake.

"You've not attended a party like this before with your companion?" Darryx asked.

"My sister and no," Jake replied glancing into the crowd to see if he could see her.

"Interesting place to bring your... twin sister," Darryx said.

"She wanted to check out the party and dragged me along." Jake shrugged.

"Still, not many siblings at a party like this," Darryx said.

Jake frowned and turned around to ask Darryx about the party but the man seemed to have stepped away suddenly. Jake looked around for him, but didn't see him anywhere.

"Can't say I'm going to miss the pervert," Jake mumbled and took a drink of the soda.

After about fifteen minutes of searching, Jake found his sister chatting up two young men in prime physical condition who seemed more interested in her body than her conversation. Jenna giggled upon seeing him.

"Hey bro!" she said as she hugged him. She turned back to the other men and pointed at them, squinting. "These guys are... damn, I forgot your names already!"

"Yeah, that happens at Darryx's parties," the taller blonde man replied with a laugh.

All around them, Jake and Jenna could see the partygoers getting more than a little friendly with each other. Some of them were making out and Jake swore he saw a couple of men disappear into another room, one holding the other's hand. Jake wondered how Caligula it might get and swallowed nervously.

The music suddenly came to a halt and everyone's attention swerved to a large fireplace where Darryx stood holding up his hands. Jenna and Jake followed everyone's gaze.

"We have a special occasion tonight!" Darryx

announced. "We have twins attending the party! Jake and Jenna, could you come forward please?"

Jake was concerned that this man knew their names. He didn't remember giving them when they met. For some reason, worry faded almost as quickly as it came. Jake and Jenna moved forward feeling almost in a haze as they did so. Hands touched and groped them as they moved forward. In a normal setting, Jake would be furious, but at the moment, he couldn't find a reason to object. He almost enjoyed the attention.

As soon as they reached the fireplace, they stood transfixed looking into Darryx's eyes. They felt warmth and trust, like he'd always been their friend and knew what was best.

"Don't you think we should do something special with our new friends? Something befitting their special status?" Darryx asked the crowd.

The gathered masses shouted their encouragement again and again. Jake and Jenna stood as if drugged, gently swaying in place. Darryx raised his hands and the crowd quieted down.

"In honor of the bond they share as twins, a very special bond, I pronounce they will consummate their relationship," Darryx said as he stared into their eyes. "Alec and Bryce take them to the master suite upstairs and stand guard outside. I don't want their special night to be disturbed."

The two young men Jenna had chatted with earlier grabbed the two siblings as they gazed at each other in wonder, as if seeing the other for the first time. Alec, the blonde, pulled Jenna ahead to the grand staircase. Bryce had his hand on Jake's arm, but didn't have to do much as he followed his sister eagerly in his trancelike state.

The grand staircase was wide enough to go two by two, and the pairs ascended quickly to the second story. The thumping music resumed and vibrated the floor below their feet. Alec and Bryce moved efficiently through the hall to a large bedroom suite to the left. The double doors were open and they walked the entranced siblings into the bed chamber. Letting go of their charges, Alec and Bryce retreated from the room, closing the doors as the brother and sister embraced.

Clearly not themselves, they shared a long, passionate kiss. When they broke it off, Jenna looked into Jake's eyes and whispered "Take off your clothes."

Only too happy to oblige, Jake stepped back and removed his shirt. When he got to the tight pants, his unfamiliarity with the clothing put him off balance and he fell to the floor, whacking his head on one of the columns of the four poster bed. He grabbed his head and cursed silently, gritting his teeth. When he opened his eyes, it felt like a mist was lifted. His mind cleared and he grimaced. He'd just shared an impassioned kiss with his sister. That was going to take a while to forget.

He looked back up at his sister and gasped. She had stripped bare and was humming softly, swaying back and forth. He put his hand up on the bed and a cloud of dust burst into the air. Coughing roughly, Jake stood back up, pulling his pants back together.

Jenna walked up to him and tried to get his pants undone again. She was still under whatever spell Darryx had placed on them. Jake grabbed his sister by the shoulders, gingerly avoiding her bare breasts.

"Please forgive me," he said and slapped her across the face soundly enough to whip her head to the side but not break anything. She immediately grabbed her face.

Jake stood waiting for her to break out of it. Instead, she turned and smiled.

"Oh, I like it rough," Jenna smirked.

"Oh great," Jake said. Then he kicked her in the shin and she dropped to the floor.

"Ow, what'd you do that for, creep?" Jenna growled and then caught her breath. She fell back onto her butt, covering herself with her hands. "Oh my God, Jake..."

"Keep it down, your two paramours are outside

the door," Jake hissed. Jenna glanced at the door and then back at Jake.

"Mmm, yes, I like it just like that," Jenna murmured sexily as she scrambled to grab her clothes. "Yes, suck it!"

"Mmm," Jake rumbled loudly. Jenna quickly put her clothes back on as they continued making cooing sounds. Jake slid his shirt back on while he checked out the room. The bathroom was huge but a dead end. There were also two French doors leading out to a balcony. The music was so loud in the house that they couldn't hear their two guards if they'd been talking, but it also meant they were less likely to be heard exploring and hopefully escaping.

"What do we do?" Jenna whispered when she'd put her clothes back on.

Jake approached the French doors and opened them slowly. The music got a bit louder, but Jake didn't think the guards would hear the difference. He stepped to the edge of the balcony and assessed the drop.

"We can make it down. We'll just have to hang from the edge and drop down. It's only one floor." Jake whispered. Jenna nodded and the two of them climbed to the other side of the railing, worked their way to just hanging on the edge of the balcony with their hands and then dropped to the ground below.

In the dim light provided by the moon struggling to peek through the clouds overhead, they could see a tall hedge blocked their way to the front of the house and a tall stone fence surrounded the extensive back yard of the huge estate.

"They don't make it easy to escape, do they?" Jenna hissed.

"Maybe the back of the fence isn't solid or there's a gate somewhere," Jake replied. "Come on."

They felt their way along the house and within a few feet, the composition of the structure changed considerably. They squinted at the house and it had changed to a stone construction, one that looked and felt like it had aged for centuries.

"What the hell?" Jake whispered. They continued forward until the ground suddenly gave way beneath their feet.

Landing on the cold stone floor ten feet down knocked the wind out of both of them. They struggled to breathe as musty, damp ancient air filled their lungs. They both rolled onto their sides and coughed until they could draw a clear enough breath to regain their senses. The dim light from above did little to illuminate their surroundings. Aside from the broken rotted wood underneath and around them, they couldn't see much. Jake felt in his back pocket and pulled out his cell phone.

There was no signal, but he used the light to get some idea of the lay of the room.

"You okay?" Jake coughed out.

"Yeah, nothing broken, but plenty bruised including my face thanks to you," Jenna said.

"At least you didn't break your sense of humor," Jake replied. He stood on shaky feet and peered into the gloom. "Just seems to be a big basement. Really old though."

"What's that thing in the corner?" Jenna pointed to a corner far across the room where a faint light shone on one of the walls. Jake helped Jenna to her feet.

"Maybe it's the light from a door that will take us out of here," Jake said as he guided them through the dark room with his light pointed at the floor.

They could still hear the music through the broken opening they'd fallen through. But within a few moments, it stopped and shouting voices could be heard. They couldn't make out what was being said, but they had a pretty good idea that their escape was no longer secret.

"Dammit," Jenna said as she looked behind them.

"Can't be helped. Let's see if this is a way out," Jake said, still holding her hand and pulling her along with him toward the glow in the corner. As they got closer to the corner, they noticed debris on the stone floor. It became more distinct in shape and form until they realized it was small bones. The further they got, the larger the bones became until they both stopped. A mere ten feet from the glowing wall, an unmistakable human skull stared at them from the ground. Bits of moss, dirt or possibly flesh clung to the pitted surface, giving it depth and definition.

"Find them!" The dark voice of Darryx rang out from above, yelling at what they assumed were the partygoers. "Or you'll suffer the same fate as Alec and Bryce!"

Jake and Jenna looked at each other in shock. They slowly looked back down at the skull staring up at them. They continued moving forward.

With every step, the frequency of human remains increased until they were literally pushing bones aside with their feet to press forward. Finally, they reached a glowing orb embedded in the floor. Arrayed around the orb were the bones of hands stretched toward the orb, as if they'd touched it and had the flesh burned away in an instant.

"Augh!" came the anguished scream of Darryx from near the broken hole. "I'll cleave the flesh from your bones myself!"

They heard his feet hit the broken wood behind them. They looked at each other and reached for the orb.

"Stop!" Darryx commanded and the twins found themselves unable to move, not wanting to move and just wanting to obey their beloved master. From somewhere in the dark mass of bones, two skulls flew from the dusty graves and struck the twins in the side of their heads hard. They blinked as the spell of Darryx's mesmerizing voice was temporarily broken by forces unseen.

They reached out quickly and touched the orb simultaneously.

Instantly, they screamed in pain, feeling white hot fire burning them from the inside out.

Darryx chuckled a dark, wet laugh.

"You'll die just like the others, a phosphorous clump of shiny bones!" Darryx shouted to the sky.

The twins turned to look at him. Their eyes glowed a greenish white with the fire of a hundred souls. The pain turned into warmth and a feeling of pure energy.

"This time will be different," they said in unison, their voices an eerie hollow sound of dozens of voices echoing within the room.

"What?" Darryx took a step back. "No!"

Darryx rushed the twins with a growl, but they held their hands in front of them and hundreds of shards of broken bones flew through the air, striking Darryx as if he was a pin cushion. It drove him back against the wall where he screamed out in pain. Blood oozed from multiple wounds.

"You think this pathetic attack will defeat me?" Darryx screamed and he staggered against the wall. "I've lived a thousand lifetimes crushing pathetic weaklings like you!"

"We won't defeat you, Darryx," the twins said in unison as they picked up the orb. "You'll be judged by the hundreds of souls you've tormented."

The remaining bones in the room, tens of thousands in all, rose from the ground and pummeled the master. They piled around him, pinning him against the wall, confining his limbs until only his face remained visible.

"You'll be destroyed by the power you stole from her," the twins said as they walked forward and placed the orb on his forehead.

At first, Darryx laughed. But the laughter turned to blood curdling screams as every soul he'd tormented began to cut his own soul to pieces. The screaming brought Darryx's acolytes. One by one, they dropped down the hole. Instead of coming to his aid, however, they all lined up against the far wall, sat down and watched with grim fascination.

"Help me, you bastards!" Darryx screamed.

As one, his followers droned, "You're no longer the master."

Finally, the orb claimed his physical body and every cell of Darryx' body erupted in white hot flame. He only felt the pain of a thousand suns for an instant before he was nothing more than dust amongst the pile of bones.

Jake and Jenna dropped the orb and it fell into the pile of bones, disappearing from sight. They turned to look at the partygoers all lined up against the wall. The mesmerized gaggle of young people prostrated themselves before the twins.

"Mistress and master, your wish is our command."

# CRAWLIES

**D**octor Melanie Harris maneuvered the computer controlled scalpel down the abdomen of the microscopic bug. Her eyes strained at the ocular lenses as she rapidly blinked, trying to force sleep from her eyes. The incision revealed the tiny bulbs in the insect's abdomen, connected by a small duct that had to be the combination chamber for the compounds within the bulbs.

"That's the only mystery to solve—how those compounds are combined," Melanie said.

Behind her, crouched over a keyboard typing frantically and moving his mouse around, her lab partner, Doctor Felix Gorun grunted.

"We're close, Felix," Melanie replied and she sat back in the chair and rubbed her eyes. "I just need a break. We're going to make mistakes and miss something if we're too tired to function."

"We don't have that luxury!" Felix growled. "We need more samples."

"We've got a hundred of the little buggers," Melanie sighed. "That'll have to do until the next shipment clears quarantine."

"She'll die by then," Felix whispered.

Melanie groaned and stood up.

"I'm sorry, there's only so much we can do," Melanie said. "If we can get this solved, we might be able to synthesize what she needs. But I've got to get some sleep."

"I understand, Melanie. Go get some sleep," Felix said. "I'll see you in a few hours."

She walked up to him and put a comforting hand on his shoulder.

"You should get some sleep too," Melanie said. "Coffee can only do so much."

"I will." Felix nodded. "I'm close to a breakthrough. I can feel it."

"Okay," Melanie said. "I'm too tired to argue or ask."

Melanie walked out of the room and the door shut slowly behind her. The door clicked and Felix turned around. He looked at the clock on the wall. It was 4 AM.

In a swift motion, Felix walked to the door and

looked through the small window. He saw Melanie through the larger plate glass door leading outside getting into her car. He watched as she turned on the car and pulled out of the parking lot. He waited until her car drove out of sight.

Felix locked the door and walked across the lab. He opened the specimen cabinet and slid a tray with fifty of the microscopic bugs out of the containment box. He stopped for a moment at his computer to double check the specific isotope that engendered mutation in this species and then took the tray with him into the protective chamber. He placed the tray on the counter, put on lead lined gloves, took a small vial, put it next to the tray and removed the stopper from the top. He marked a ten second exposure on the wall clock and put the stopper back in.

After returning all materials to their proper location, he sat back down at his computer and messaged Arnold, his research assistant. The reply came back a few minutes later. Arnold was groggy but he'd be at Felix's home shortly.

Felix gave a sigh. He typed into his computer and brought up a live video feed. There on a bed in a nearby hospital, lay his wife Irene. She had tubes running under the blankets, into her mouth and nose. Machines flashed and monitoring machines tracked every vital sign she possessed. Irene clung to life in an ever deteriorating state.

Felix touched the monitor for a moment, his eyes a mirror to his soul, reflecting the pain and loss he felt even though she wasn't gone yet. Desperation tore at his very fiber, wanting, hoping for a last minute cure to regenerate what she had lost. He would do anything to bring her back from the brink of death.

Felix grabbed a specimen bag, walked to the specimen cabinet and placed the irradiated tray in the bag. He zipped it closed and walked out the door.

Within minutes, Felix pulled up in front of the Tudor mansion he shared with his stricken wife, a three story sprawling affair that spanned over twelve thousand square feet. It was the spoils of two decades of medical research successes and profiteering from the various cures and treatments of the very ill. Insane markups on life saving procedures filled not just Felix's coffers but also those of his investors. He'd made a very tidy sum treating illness but very rarely curing anything. Keep the patient alive and milk them for every penny they have, that was the only way to ensure an endless flow of cash. Cure them and the money spigot turned off quickly.

But he'd gotten lazy. After years of developing 'almost' cures, extended treatment protocols and never curing a damn thing, his skills had atrophied. His once brilliant mind was hitting dead ends, wandering down directionless pathways searching for a cure to a rare condition no one had ever researched because it was never cost effective, could never bring a hefty reward for the investment required. Now, in his hour of need, he was going to have to cut a few corners to get the end result he needed.

Felix placed the specimen tray in the internal delivery system of the containment chamber. One small charge would shatter the tray, releasing the specimens within. The enclosed recirculation system would do the rest, delivering the microscopic bugs to their target, beginning the life cycle to create more. He only hoped a single body could produce enough of them to create a cure.

He placed several boxes of notes within the containment unit—the bait to get Arnold in there. The groggier his assistant was, the better for his purposes. He made sure there was nothing hard enough to damage the containment unit from the inside. Cardboard and paper would do little to rupture the plastics and silicone polymers sealing the small room. It was designed to contain a small primate who might get out of control, a way to contain the infection while at the same time allowing for samples to be taken from the contained environment. It had been designed for bioweapon testing, but the funding had run dry before he could ever put it to use away from prying eyes. Now he was grateful for the advanced funding and secret construction. Few were aware of the room beneath his mansion and none of those who did cared.

Felix double checked the video systems within the unit. He could track every square inch of the interior, watch the genesis of the infestation, and track its progress. He hoped it wouldn't take long to come to fruition. After he made sure everything was in order, he sat in his chair waiting, fretting. He looked at the clock, knowing Arnold would be there within a few minutes. He absently twirled his wedding ring and his thoughts wandered to his bride and their many years of matrimony. Of all the places they'd traveled over these two decades together, she'd loved the French Riviera the best. They stayed in Monaco and ventured out to Paris, Italy and Spain, but always came back to that little principality. Evenings by the Mediterranean sipping wine and dining on fresh fish were the simplest of pleasures she enjoyed the most. Her laughter was the breath of life he treasured above all else. He glanced at the chamber across the basement and realized this was the only option to bring her back anywhere near her former self.

"Doc?" came Arnold's sleepy voice, struggling with a yawn. "You down here?"

Felix set his fingers to tapping at the computer, bringing up simulations of medical trials he'd been working on with Arnold over the last few weeks.

"Down here, Arnold," Felix called out. "I've just got a few more simulations to run, but I need someone keeping track and working the research for me. We're in the home run, I can feel it."

"You got it, Doc," Arnold said as he walked into the room. His hands went through his unruly brown curls. "I know how you get when you're on a roll."

Arnold looked around the room. Various boxes were arrayed across the tables and benches, some papers spilled out from the boxes and had fallen on the floor.

"It's been a while since we've been down here," Arnold said. "Clearly the maid hasn't visited either."

"If you could tidy up while I'm finishing this. Oh, I think there are some notes and things in the containment unit as well. I might need those next," Felix said.

"Sure thing," Arnold said as he walked into the containment unit and grabbed the first box. Felix was on his feet and at the huge containment door in a second. The well oiled door swung shut with a clang as Felix locked it down, engaging the seal.

Inside the unit, Arnold frowned. He set the box down and went to the door. It had been designed to be locked from the outside. He searched the sides of the door for a release mechanism, but there wasn't one.

"Doc?!" Arnold shouted. "This isn't funny! I get claustrophobic!"

The sound of glass breaking caused Arnold's head to swivel to the other side of the small containment unit. The circulation system began moving air within the confined space.

"No," Arnold's eyes got wide. He turned back to the door and pounded on it with all his strength. "Doc! What's going on! What's in here?!"

Outside the chamber, Felix' eyes were glued to the video system showing Arnold pounding on the door. He leaned forward as Arnold began to scratch the skin on his exposed arms and neck. He zoomed in to watch the skin redden and then heal, redden again and then heal again. The cycle repeated over and over again.

Inside the chamber, Arnold howled in pain as his skin continually ruptured on a microscopic level and then healed over. The bugs consumed his flesh in small microscopic bits, expelled a healing antidote to keep the flesh from reacting, and then bred. Arnold watched in horror as his skin changed color in a fast moving wave, showing the rapid progression of the mites spreading across his body. The skin reddening advanced to bubbling after a few minutes as he fell to the floor writing in pain, his throat hoarse from screaming. After about fifteen minutes, he stopped moving and his flesh began to wither away, consumed by the feeding frenzy of the microscopic bugs in their advanced speed lifecycle.

Felix walked over to the containment unit, his face grim. Arnold had been a good assistant, but sacrifices had to be made. He stepped up to the sample portal and placed a sealed vial over the small nozzle. He pressed a button and contaminated air entered the vial. Felix walked back to his desk and placed the vial under an ultraviolet light; the air inside the vial swarmed with activity, millions of microscopic bugs cavorted inside the little tube.

"Yes!" Felix shouted. He pressed a few buttons and an ultraviolet light went on inside the containment unit. The air was alive with movement. Felix jumped up and danced around shouting and laughing.

"Arnold!" he shouted to the ceiling. "Your sacrifice was not in vain!"

Felix returned to the desk and placed the vial under a microscope. The lens was filled by the cascading waves of microscopic bugs which, under magnification, seemed to have grown larger and...

Felix sat back from the microscope and rubbed his eyes. He looked into the ocular lenses again and frowned. The insects now had wings. He got up and walked over to the containment cube. Through the thick glass, he could still see Arnold's skeleton stripped clean of all flesh through the purple haze of a glowing mist that was millions of flying, burrowing insects hungry for their next meal. Felix absently twirled his wedding ring as he stared at the undulating mist. As he stared, he recognized patterns in their flight. The bugs were communicating as if through a hive mind, or maybe telepathically. How many generations of mutations had they gone through in this accelerated evolution. What had he created?

Felix walked quickly to his computer and uploaded his research to the cloud. It would be incriminating if someone breached it, but the danger of not having this data was too great to not risk it. He put the vial with the bug sample into another, larger sealed case and walked out of the room, but not before he heard the alarm sound; the containment unit had been breached. If the insects could breach that... Felix ran from the room and up the stairs.

At the top of the stairs, Felix slammed the basement door shut and hit the emergency containment button, sealing the room below him. Inside the basement, a thick gas streamed into the room and a spark ignited the cloud, engulfing the room in flames. A secondary nozzle sprayed oxygen into the room to keep the fire going, burning everything to a cinder. As the heat reached over 1600 degrees, the metal inside the room began to liquefy.

Felix climbed into his car and drove away from the mansion at top speed. The nearest neighbors were nearly a mile away. When he cleared the front gate, the basement collapsed and the building behind him exploded. In the rearview mirror, he watched as the skeleton frame of the building, engulfed in flames, struggled to stay standing.

Felix scratched his head.

"Dang dandruff..." he said as he continued down the road. The itching in his scalp intensified to a pain. The pain traveled down his neck. He looked at his hand as it began to scratch too. He recognized the red skin irritation.

"Shit."

Felix turned the car around. He called Melanie's phone. It rang until voicemail answered. Of course, she was still asleep after a long night. No one else he could turn to. No time.

"Melanie, this is Felix. I've made a terrible mistake," Felix said. He gritted his teeth as the pain in his skull increased. Focusing through the pain, Felix kept his car on the road and barreled toward his burning home. He gave Melanie the details on how to access his digital records in the clouds.

"They won't explain why, but I think you already know," Felix said as he accelerated past his front gate, the inferno in front of his eyes wavered—a combination of the heat blurring the air and the insects burrowing into his brain matter. "I'm sorry."

In the milliseconds he had before descending into Hades, Felix's brain seized on his happiest memories of Irene accompanied by a wistfulness for that which would never come to pass.

Felix's car plowed into the side of the flaming wreckage and disappeared inside. A few seconds later, the ruptured gas tank exploded, adding a small ball of fire to the rising flames and smoke.

Two hours later, Melanie woke to a pounding on her door. Before she could get out of bed, the door was busted open and an army of U.S. Marshals swarmed into her apartment. When they found her, guns drawn, one of the female Marshals held a photograph up and compared it to Melanie.

"Doctor Melanie Harris? You need to come with us. National emergency."

Melanie clutched her sheets around her.

"I sleep in the nude…"

"About face!" the woman shouted and the men

all turned around. "Out, so she has some privacy."

The men in the room filed out. The woman stayed in the room with Melanie.

"You've got five minutes and then we're leaving. Dress warm," the woman said and then went to stand by the door, still inside and clearly not leaving. She had the courtesy to not follow Melanie with her eyes, but maintained a calm, detached stare at the wall behind Melanie's bed. Melanie jumped up and pulled on underclothes, sweats and tennis shoes.

"Ready," Melanie replied. "What's this about?"

"The US is under attack," the woman replied as she led Melanie out by the arm. "You may be the only person who can save us."

Melanie was taken to a black, unmarked SUV and pushed in roughly. The car took off immediately, speeding down roads which had been cleared of traffic. As Melanie looked out the window, she saw police at every intersection stopping traffic. They had guns drawn.

The SUV raced to the local high school where a helicopter sat in the athletic field. The rotors slowly rotated as it waited for Melanie. The vehicle drove onto the field directly to the waiting chopper. Melanie was escorted out and handed off to the military personnel waiting for her. She climbed in, the door shut and they lifted into the air swiftly.

"Flight path clear, heading south," Melanie heard the pilot say. A man with dark hair in a suit was nestled among the soldiers in khaki uniforms. He nodded his head toward Melanie.

"Doctor Harris?" the man asked. "I'm Director Salazar."

"Director, what's going on?"

"Your colleague, Doctor Felix Gorun is dead," Director Salazar said. "I'll give you a moment to process that information, so we can continue."

Melanie looked at the floor of the helicopter feeling like she'd been punched in the gut.

"I just saw him a few hours ago. Now he's dead?" Melanie felt like she was going to throw up. She wasn't sure if it was the flight or the news or maybe a combination of both. Director Salazar handed her a vomit bag.

"I'll be fine," she said, pushing it away. Director Salazar kept the bag close.

"You're going to need it after you see this," he said as he handed her a small computer tablet. Melanie looked up at Director Salazar with a frown. She took the bag and then grabbed the tablet. On the screen, the little arrow waiting for a touch to start the video stared at her like a viper waiting to strike. She placed the tablet on her lap, adjusted the screen and started the video. She kept the bag handy.

What played for Melanie was a cut together version of events, starting with footage from the lab she shared with Felix and ending with grainy satellite footage of Felix's home exploding and Felix driving into the wreckage. She vomited twice—first when Arnold died and second when Felix did.

Director Salazar handed her a damp cloth to clean up with and took the tablet back.

"First responders to the fire passed away within twenty minutes of arrival at Dr. Gorun's residence. Lost a few waves of them before we cordoned off the area. We've sent in drones, but they've been disabled a few hundred yards into the quarantine zone. We've used some other methods to try to get a handle on what's going on. The quarantine zone is growing. Whatever Dr. Gorun created, released or whatever is growing and expanding. What do you know?"

"We were doing research on a small mite recently discovered in the Amazon. It had healing properties we were trying to unlock." Melanie put her hand to her mouth. "To save his wife. He was trying to save his wife!"

"That's what we suspected when we went over the controlled substances records," Director Salazar said. "But those insects have a limited infection area and he destroyed his lab where they were."

Director Salazar tapped on the tablet a few times and handed it back to Melanie.

"He sent you a voicemail and told you to look at the records. We don't have the right personnel to interpret this on site yet. Speed is of the essence."

Melanie scrolled through the records of the experiment Felix was performing and a sick sense of dread settled in her stomach.

"Speed is the problem," Melanie said. "He treated the original specimens with a particular type of radiation to promote their mutation. I think he was trying to get them to grow faster. Instead, he created a runaway mutation. They sped up their life cycle and evolved with each generation."

"So they can fly now," Director Salazar said.

"More than that," Melanie said. "He theorized they can communicate with each other and act like a hive mind. Who knows what they'll evolve to next... or already have? Director, if these calculations are correct, they've evolved at a faster rate than the human species."

"It's only been five hours," Director Salazar chided.

"He accelerated their life cycle and the rate at which mutations would occur. In an hour, they would've changed hundreds of times. They've gone through thousands of years of evolution in just a few hours."

"We've gone through millions of years," Director Salazar said. "What does it matter?"

"If they've also mutated at the same rate we have up until now, this could put them ahead of us in the evolutionary chain. Think of what humans could be in several thousand years from now. These insects have already leaped ahead of us and they're continuing to do so."

"How do we stop them?"

Melanie shook her head.

"We have to stop them, Dr. Harris."

"How do you stop what you can't even see?" Melanie said. "They could be in this helicopter observing, waiting to decide what to do to us next. We've already lost."

"You can't say we've already lost after five hours. Give me something better."

Melanie sat back in her seat as the helicopter banked. She went over the different scenarios in her mind. Nothing made sense. How could Felix do this? He cleared knew he'd messed up. Mankind had devised its own end.

"I'm sure you've considered nuclear options," Melanie said.

"It's been floated. When we looked at the data briefly, we saw radiation had been applied and they'd survived. There was some concern about increasing mutations or giving them a stronger immunity to a last ditch response."

"They developed in the Amazon where it's hot and humid. Cold maybe? Dehydration? Could we freeze them out or dry them up somehow?" Melanie shrugged her shoulders. "I'm sorry; I'm a medical doctor not a weapons scientist."

"Let me see what we can do," Director Salazar replied. He held his finger to his ear and looked out the window.

The helicopter landed and Melanie looked at where they'd landed, but didn't recognize anything. They were in a small clearing in the middle of a forest on a helicopter pad. There was a small building with a single door just a few hundred feet away.

The doors to the helicopter opened and two of the soldiers helped Melanie exit. Director Salazar walked ahead and they all followed him to the small building. The door opened as Director Salazar approached. A single soldier armed with an automatic rifle stood at the open door. They walked through the door into a waiting elevator.

The ride down was short but somber. Director Salazar was silent and grim. Melanie used the time to reflect on the pain Felix must have been in to resort to such a serious measure. She reflected on the times she'd seen him staring silently at the computer watching his wife as she lay in the hospital bed slowly dying. Melanie never thought he'd risk killing everyone on the planet just to save his wife. Clearly, he hadn't thought through the dangers of his activities. Perhaps he was so tired, he couldn't comprehend the damage he could do with a single experiment. But then, he'd killed Arnold. Cold blooded, calculated murder committed just on the chance it would save his wife. Perhaps, she never knew Felix at all.

A few minutes passed and the doors opened on a large room with a huge set of screens on two walls. The majority of the screens showed graphics of New York State and surrounding area. A large red circle was just east of Ithaca, where the Felix's house was located. Melanie had no real sense of the scale of the red circle, but surely it was miles in diameter.

A four-star general walked up to Director Salazar. They both shared a grim face. The general looked at Melanie.

"Thank you for coming, Doctor Harris. Follow me," the general said and they walked away from the room into a smaller conference room just down the hall to the right. Melanie recognized a few people from the science community. One of them, an Indian professor from Penn State, Dr. Mangal, was a noted entomologist. He was dressed in just a sleeping gown but he had an army khaki jacket on.

"We've just ordered a mandatory evacuation of Ithaca," the general said to the room.

"Pointless," Doctor Mangal said.

The general scowled at Doctor Mangal.

"Well, what would you have us do, Doctor?" the general grumbled as he walked to the head of the room.

"Pray to whatever gods you worship and ask for mercy," Doctor Mangal replied without missing a beat. "You've weaponized insects and now you're surprised by the outcome?"

"This wasn't a government project," the general replied.

"So you say," Doctor Mangal sat stoically, staring at the general. "Who provided the funds for Doctor Gorun to build a facility to grow this danger into a weapon?"

"His experiments were not under our direction this time. He was privately funded."

"It doesn't matter who created the problem or how," Melanie interrupted. "If this is who we have available to solve this, we need to come together and not bicker. Surely, Doctor Mangal, you understand the danger here."

Doctor Mangal looked at her and nodded.

"Surely you understand the futility of trying to put the genie back in the bottle, Doctor…?" Doctor Mangal replied.

"This is Doctor Harris, Doctor Gorun's associate," the general responded.

"How much did they pay you for weaponizing mites, Doctor Harris?" Doctor Mangal said.

"Doctor Gorun was funding the entire project himself. He was trying to find a cure for his wife," Melanie replied.

"Well, if it was to cure her from living, he succeeded," Doctor Mangal said.

"This is not productive," Director Salazar said. "Regardless of how we got here, we need to find solutions."

"How we got here has everything to do with finding a solution," Doctor Mangal replied. He nodded. "But I acknowledge the original motivation isn't relevant, just galling."

"Unfortunately, Doctor Gorun isn't here to give us firsthand knowledge," Melanie said. "His research mentioned a specific isotope that caused mutation. Wouldn't that imply other types could be deadly? I really hate to say this, but couldn't we drop a bomb outside Ithaca and wipe them out?"

"You're assuming they've remained inside the quarantine zone," Doctor Mangal said. "As I've told these bureaucrats, they've missed the mark. Something with intelligence, possibly smarter than us, would've hitched a ride out of there, on a dog or deer or even birds. Their assumption that it won't travel faster than four or five miles an hour is asinine."

"Natural predators from the Amazon?" Melanie asked. This was so far outside her realm of expertise that she was getting desperate.

"If this had been an outbreak of normal insects, that would be a brilliant option," Doctor Mangal said. He stood up and walked to the general. "What none of you seem to grasp is this is the equivalent of a zombie outbreak. Imagine the worst scenario and then multiply it by a factor of one thousand. This moves faster than a virus, faster than a zombie, faster even than an invading army."

A man in a tan suit next to Director Salazar stood up. Melanie couldn't read his name tag, but the frown on Director Salazar's face told her all she needed to know. Doctor Mangal had hit close to the truth, perhaps closer than even he realized.

"Thank you for your assessment, Doctor Mangal," the man in the dark suit said. "We have obtained an air sample from the affected area. We had some of the mutated species in a sealed container."

"Had?" Melanie blurted out.

"Forgive me, Doctor Harris and the rest of my esteemed colleagues. I should've introduced myself. Daniel Molton, Deputy Secretary of Homeland Security." Daniel gave a slight nod to the room and then raised a remote and turned on a wall sized monitor. The wall showed a map of the United States, but it included a large red circle around Atlanta, Georgia as well as a thick red line between Ithaca and Atlanta.

"Unfortunately, Doctor Mangal was only partially correct. Turns out a high speed scientific drone can spread the infection faster than any land or air creature."

Director Salazar stood up and walked to the wall. He noticed smaller red circles around major cities within two hundred miles of Ithaca. He turned to Daniel.

"You've confirmed this?"

"What you can't see, you can't stop from getting aboard an aircraft. Some of the planes landed and released the contaminant directly into the airports and surrounding areas. Others, well, the planes crashed but reports of outbreaks on the ground confirm everything beyond our worst nightmares. We ran the numbers based on Doctor Gorun's rough estimations from his notes. There are now trillions of the insects spread across the majority of the Eastern U.S. Even without our ill-conceived research drone, the infection has spread faster than anyone anticipated, faster than we could account for."

Perhaps it was a mix of lack of sleep, the death of her colleague and news too overwhelming to bear—Melanie fainted.

When she awoke, Doctor Mangal was tending to her. He'd retrieved a handkerchief from somewhere, gotten it wet and had pressed it to her forehead. Behind him, people around the room were shouting angrily about countermeasures and quarantines.

"What can we do?" Melanie asked. Doctor Mangal shook his head.

"The right thing to do would be nuclear Armageddon, blanketing the North American continent immediately," Doctor Mangal said. "They'll never authorize it. They'll try to move to bunkers, huddle down underground until the danger passes. And that, my dear, is how the human race ends."

"All is lost? Surely there must be something…" Melanie felt faint again and Doctor Mangal caught her head before it dropped hard to the floor.

"Within hours, the infestation will spread to every corner of the globe. They'll keep it a state secret to avoid panic which will only aid in the spread. If they'd nuked Ithaca five hours ago…" He shook his head. "No, probably not even then. I looked at the notes your colleague left behind. I saw the destruction of the facility, his home. He did everything he could to stop it and it was already too late by the time he realized what had happened."

"What about inoculations?"

"Against what?" Doctor Mangal patted her hand. "We have no samples, no dead bodies to examine, no real idea what the insects have mutated into. Even if we had all that, by the time we developed a vaccine, they would've already mutated beyond its reach. Assuming we had even that much time."

"Mosquito spraying?" Melanie whispered.

"Very specific to mosquito larvae. Not enough of it stockpiled to stop the spread even if it worked."

Doctor Mangal turned to look at the wall and saw the spread of the infestation had reached across the Mississippi and was working its way West. The computer projections showed the Eastern seaboard was solid red.

"Humanity had a good run," Doctor Mangal said. Absently, he scratched his neck.

# PENANCE

**B**radley Whitmer slowly opened his eyes. Light filtered in through his lids, illuminating his world at the same speed as the pain in his hands. He tried to move them, but that only made the searing pain worse. As his senses awoke, the first thing to reach past the pain was the awful smell. Dead flesh rotted somewhere nearby and the odor was overwhelming. Bradley realized the smell would be worse if he had both nostrils clear, but something blocked his right nostril. Whatever it was, he could feel it rubbing inside his nasal cavity and tickling the back of his throat.

Finally, his eyes adjusted to the light and he gasped at what he saw. Laid out on a table a few feet away was his old buddy, Norman. He looked at Norman's broken body. His hands had holes caked with blood and darker substances. His feet were completely black as though stricken by frostbite. On various parts of his body, there were abrasions, bruises and possibly burns, but the most disturbing were the various wounds—small holes that had a trail of blood leading from them.

Bradley tried moving his legs, but they were held in place by something. He realized his feet hurt. He didn't know how long he'd been trapped in this standing position, but he could feel the muscles in his back and legs aching already. Realizing he couldn't move or even see what was holding him in place, he did the only rational thing his mind could formulate.

"Help! Somebody help me!" Bradley shouted.

"Ah, you're awake. Excellent. Be with you in a moment," a woman's voice announced over a speaker somewhere in the room.

Bradley tried turning his head, but it was held firmly in place by some kind of straps, braced by some kind of cold and hard bars. Bradley imagined it was a steel cage of some sort. He tried to look down, but only saw the edge of a metal plate. His chin couldn't move down due to some kind of padded bar or shelf.

A door across the room opened, bringing with it a slight breeze to his lower extremities. It was at this point he realized his body was completely exposed, at least the part that wasn't flush against the back of this cage he was in.

The woman who walked in was of average height.

The track lighting overhead accompanied by a small single light bulb in the center of the room showed she was a blonde or possibly dirty blonde, Bradley thought. She was moderately attractive, although she was clearly in her early forties or something. Not the kind of woman he'd normally hit on. Way too old. Still, if he could seduce her into letting him go, he'd make the sacrifice.

"Hey, sweetheart," he said. "Can you let me loose? Somebody's trapped me in here! Please, I'll do anything you want."

The woman looked up at Bradley and the gaze was cold and calculating. There was no warmth, no empathy for his situation. She merely acknowledged she'd heard the words and then stepped over to a small cabinet next to the door. He watched her pull out a small container, dip her fingers in it and wipe the substance across her upper lip just under her nose.

"It really stinks in here," she mused. "May need to get the maid to clean this up."

She laughed at her own joke and picked up a hammer from inside the cabinet. She raised the hammer and brought it down with tremendous force in the center of Norman's chest.

"Jesus!" Bradley exclaimed.

"Oh, not to worry," she said. "Your friend Norman here is quite dead. I was just releasing a little tension."

"What the hell," Bradley cried out. "Who killed him?"

"Hmm," the woman said. "You know, it's possible you could consider Norman's death a suicide. You see, he refused to tell me where you and he buried my daughter's body after you raped and strangled her. No matter what I did to his physical body, he seemed to be unwilling to let loose of that information."

"I don't know what the hell you're talking about!" Bradley screamed. "We didn't do anything!"

"You raped her the first time, thinking your buddy on the force would bury the evidence if she ever came forward. Then, when she did come forward, you visited her a second time, had your way with her again and killed her."

"We didn't rape anyone," Bradley said calmly. "You're mistaken. Please, just let me go and I won't tell anyone."

"Oh you'll tell someone, all right. Detective Martin Stone, if I'm not mistaken. The one who told you he'd bury the evidence. Only, he held onto it. Probably didn't trust the men raping women at random, even though you're clearly brothers in crime. I managed to get most of what he'd put aside for a rainy day and recovered my daughter's rape kit. It took some doing, but since I never intended you to face the legal system for your crimes, I didn't need to worry about chain of evidence or any stupid crap like that. Processed the kit privately and pulled the DNA I needed. I processed all of them."

She put on blue silicon gloves and approached Bradley. She grabbed his genitals and squeezed hard. Bradley screamed.

"Seems like you prefer taking your victims up the ass, Bradley. That's where they recovered your samples from."

Outside of his view, she reached for something while still holding onto his genitalia with a firm grip. He felt something slimy touch his scrotum and instinctively clenched his butt cheeks. However, the frame he was strapped to prevented him from closing his legs and whatever the device was slid without much resistance into his rectum.

"I never got to use this on Norman. Maybe I would've gotten better results," she said and stood up and walked away from Bradley. She raised a small black remote in her right hand and pressed a button.

Bradley went stiff as the electricity tore through his colon. The white hot pain robbed him of speech and he found he couldn't even breathe. His eyes were clenched shut so tightly he couldn't see anything but white spots before his eyes. Then, mercifully, everything went dark.

He raised his head sharply as the smelling salts hit his left nostril. She looked at him with disgust.

"Guess you can dish it out but you can't take it," she said and spit at his face. "Pathetic."

"Please don't do that again," Bradley whimpered.

"Really? How often did my daughter beg for mercy while you and your thug friend here ignored her pleas?" She smacked Norman's abdomen for emphasis. "Here's what I think about you begging for mercy."

She raised her hand and pressed the button again. This time, Bradley was sure he broke a tooth when he clenched his teeth before passing out. Moments later, he was awake again and screamed about the pain erupting from his mouth.

This time, she seemed to take pity on him. She walked to the cabinet and retrieved some items he couldn't see.

"Well, we can't have that distracting you from answering my questions, can we?" She said as she approached him again. "Open up and let doctor see your problem."

Bradley shook his head and clamped his mouth shut. She grabbed his genitals again and he shouted in pain. With lightning speed, she had slipped a rubber stopper of some sort into his mouth, forcing it to stay open. She pulled another piece of thick padding and shoved it against the brace around his head, immobilizing his skull. With practiced skill, she put a cap on with a light and shined it into Bradley's mouth. Bradley felt the cold steel enter his mouth as she probed the broken tooth. He felt another tool enter his mouth. She tugged on the tooth while he screamed until she pulled it out.

She smiled at him and raised a soldering iron in front of his face.

"Got to cauterize the wound," she said. He wasn't sure if it was the smell of his flesh cooking or the searing pain that erupted from his jaw that caused him to pass out again.

When he awoke again, she was examining Norman's body and cutting into it with a scalpel. Despite himself, he groaned giving away his conscious state. She glanced up at him and then back down at Norman's abdomen which lay flayed open.

"I was wondering if sepsis had caused Norman's premature death. I mean, I gave him everything I knew how to keep him alive. Then his feet went gangrene," she absently waved at Norman's blackened feet. "I was afraid this might hasten his passing. The screws were quality surgical steel and sterilized very well, so I was pretty certain I hadn't introduced an infection."

"You're crazy," Bradley said.

She looked at Bradley and smiled. "Can't

remember her name, can you? My daughter, that is. How many victims are wandering around in that little memory of yours, Bradley?"

"I haven't raped anyone," Bradley responded. She grabbed the remote and held it up.

"Fifteen," Bradley gritted out between his aching teeth.

"That is all the evidence I recovered that your good detective friend had buried. Knowing many victims fail to report their attack, I know the number is likely higher. Very cagey, Bradley. Fifteen is all you joined Norman here in attacking. I have a feeling your personal conquest number is much larger. However, I don't feel the need to punish you beyond the verifiable evidence."

She picked up a drill and walked over to Bradley.

"What are you doing?" Bradley asked, trying to put on a brave face but failing miserably.

"Where is my daughter's body, Bradley Whitmer?"

"I don't know!" Bradley shouted.

He felt the tip of the screw pierce his left quadriceps just to the side of where the bone would be. He screamed himself hoarse as the drill swiftly tore a hole in his leg and sunk the tip of the long screw into the wooden plank behind it.

"You fucking bitch!" Bradley screamed.

"There we are. Now the rapist comes to the

surface," she said. "Emma Thornberg. If you can remember your victims by their name, you just might avoid all the screws. I'll give you some time to think about it. I need a nap."

She walked away, set the drill on a small tray next to Norman's dead body and exited the room. The sharp, continuous throbbing pain in Bradley's leg brought tears to his eyes. He pulled at the restraints on his other leg and tried to dislodge his hands from where they were secured. Even with the pain from his jaw and hands, nothing detracted from the stabbing dagger of fire in his leg.

Bradley tried to sleep, rest, anything to get him through the next day or two. He realized he had no idea how long he'd been here, nor any idea how long this maniac intended to keep him. Surely they'd report him missing at work. Would they have any reason to look here? He realized his suppression of the evidence would make it unlikely anyone would even think to make the connection to Emma's mother. He wracked his brain to remember Emma, but nothing came to mind. There had been too many victims. The violence was a pleasant recollection, their screams and begging a wonderful memory, but he couldn't remember their faces. He never knew some of their names.

She'll never get the locations of their bodies from

him. Those were precious trophies and memories. He wasn't surprised Norman didn't give them up. They were of a like mind, cut from the same dark cloth. Just to the right of his field of vision, he noticed a tall contraption. A thick bar of steel ran across the middle from which the chin support appeared to be connected. The thick wooden frame visible through the openings in the steel was stained with blood, fecal material and something black. He mused that could be fluids that had darkened over time or merely darker crap Norman had pushed out during his torture. There were openings in the side which must provide access for whatever medical requirements or tortures she'd devised could be administered.

It looked like the torture cylinder was on wheels, so she must've rolled it there. He chuckled. If she thought that would add to his fear, she was sorely mistaken. When Martin didn't get his weekly check from him or Norman, he'd come looking for them. Martin knew who Emma's mother was. She wasn't as invincible or invisible as she thought she was. It was going to be a rude awakening when Martin found her; he had a mean streak darker than anything he or Norman had ever conceived of.

A whirring sound brought Bradley's attention. Behind the table on which Norman's decaying body lay, a screen rose up from a cabinet just out of view. The screen came to life and Emma's mother came into view in the kitchen above.

"Hi Bradley!" She said cheerily. "You inspired me to go shopping the other day and I just had to share the unwrapping with you."

She lifted some short handled pruning shears from the countertop and displayed them with the cardboard still tie-wrapped to the blades.

"I figured since you didn't have the figurative balls to tell me where my daughter is buried, you shouldn't have literal balls either," she smiled as she set them down. "Now, don't you worry your pretty little head. I will make them razor sharp in my little shop out back, so it will be a clean cut. Last thing I need is some loose bit of scrotal sack hanging around while I'm cauterizing the wound. Oh, that reminds me."

She walked off screen for a moment, revealing a pristinely clean kitchen. Every item placed perfectly where it belonged. She was fastidious in the kitchen even if she wasn't in the basement dungeon Bradley now called home. He tried looking at the floor; he realized it could be pristine and he'd never see it. Norman's body and the table he was on blocked the floor across the room from his view. On the screen, she walked back into view holding a dark metal rod in front of her. She held it up to the camera so he could see the flat wrought iron edge.

"I was going to have them customize it with Asshole Rapist in honor of your proclivities, but then I realized I didn't give a single fuck about you. I'm so looking forward to this, but it will have to wait. Right about now, your little detective friend should be receiving his parcel. It included a brief explanation about how we thwarted the bank security and retrieved his buried treasure from the bank. I'm not sure if he'll bother checking the bank or not, but he should be arriving soon with a ransom for the evidence we collected."

She turned her back to the camera and set the branding iron down on the counter. She cocked her head to the side for a moment and then turned back to the camera.

"Oh, did I let that slip? We. Yes, I didn't do all this alone. You'll be amazed at the amount of talent and resources you can find in fifteen sets of bereaved parents."

Bradley struggled briefly until the pain in his left thigh nearly made him pass out.

"Maybe if you shout loud enough when the detective arrives, he'll hear you and save you," she giggled. "See you soon, Bradley."

The track lighting went off leaving just the single bulb. It didn't illuminate much, but then there wasn't anything he really needed to see. Bradley closed his eyes and tried to move his right hand. Whatever pinned his hand to the board beneath, he imagined it was a long staple of some kind; he couldn't get enough leverage with the straps holding his arm, wrist and even fingers in place. He concentrated on the strap around his index finger. Between the pain and exertion, he was exhausted within a few minutes and hadn't made any progress rotating the strap that held his finger in place. For all he knew, it was secured to prevent just what he was trying to do, but he had to do something.

Bradley nodded off. He wasn't sure what time it was, but it appeared to be night outside when the knocking woke him up. On the screen, shrouded in darkness barely illuminated by a small porch light, Detective Martin Stone stood at the front door, waiting for a response to his knock.

"Come in," her voice called out and the picture changed to the kitchen. "I'm in the kitchen."

The kitchen light from the screen lit up the room Bradley waited in, the dim bulb overhead the only other illumination in the room. It seemed like a weird theater of the macabre setup just for his viewing. Bradley did the only thing he could do in the situation—shout.

"Martin! Watch out! She's crazy!" Bradley screamed at the ceiling.

On the screen, Martin walked into the kitchen and looked around the corner. She walked up behind him. Martin turned around and his eyes went wide.

"But you're dead!" he exclaimed in shock before she pulled the Taser gun from behind her back and lit him up. As Martin went down, his head struck the cabinets behind him and he was out cold. She efficiently zip tied his hands and feet, gagged his mouth and dragged him off camera.

Bradley was in shock. It didn't make sense. Martin was a seasoned officer. He should've known this was a trap. He should've been prepared. How could that happen?

She appeared shortly thereafter, opened the door to the dungeon and dragged Martin's unconscious form into the room. She closed the door and went to the cabinet with all the torture tools in it. She pulled out a syringe and a small bottle. After pulling a small dose of whatever was in the bottle into the syringe, she disappeared from Bradley's sight. He assumed she had administered some kind of tranquilizer to Martin to keep him unconscious.

As she stood up, she wiped her forehead and smiled.

"Revenge is thirsty work, Bradley," she smiled at him.

"What did he mean you were dead?" Bradley asked.

"It was a curious thing for him to say, wasn't it?" she replied. She reached behind a cabinet and a big hook on a thick chain dropped from the ceiling slowly. He hadn't noticed the winch before since it was kept out of sight. Now he knew how she was able to hoist the person or contraption upright.

"He's been on the force for fifteen years. How did you get the drop on him?" Bradley furrowed his brow. Something didn't make sense. He couldn't even remember her subduing him. How was she able to do these amazing feats?

"It's really not about Martin or Norman," she said and manipulated something behind the other torture cylinder; the wooden mount came loose. Bradley noticed the straps were secured in place by screws or brads on the back of the board. He couldn't have maneuvered them loose at all. There was also a thick steel loop secured to the back to the board. "It's all about you."

Bradley looked at her as she disappeared from sight with the board. Every once in a while, he'd see the top of her head as she maneuvered the board into place and secured Martin to it. He listened to her efforts for several minutes. Her heavy breathing eventually ended with the sound of the thick hook at the end of the chain being put into place. She stood up and walked back to the switch behind the cabinet. She clicked the switch and the winch pulled the heavy chain until it went taut. The board with Martin attached to it rose slowly from the floor.

"You enjoy torturing your victims, so what?" Bradley replied as Martin rose into view.

"Victims? Hah!" She stopped the hoist and rolled the designated torture cylinder into place. As she maneuvered Martin into place and secured the board to the cylinder, she glanced at Bradley every once in a while and laughed.

"You get off on torture," Bradley said. "I get it. The only time I really feel alive is when I'm violently dominating another human being. My preference just happens to be women. Yours is men."

"I'm nothing like you, Bradley," she said. "My joy is vengeance, pure and simple. I ask you the one question I know you'll never answer because you want to hold onto that trophy in your mind. That one body or many of them will only be yours to enjoy even unto your death."

"You're not going to do the same with my body or Norman's or Martin's?" Bradley asked.

"Bradley," she said as she picked up a scalpel from the tray beside Norman's dead body. "Whoever said I was torturing your body?"

She whipped the blade across Bradley's throat and he felt the blood trickling down his chest even as he gasped for breath. The last thing he remembered was her laughing maniacally before everything went dark.

Bradley Whitmer slowly opened his eyes. Light filtered in through his lids, illuminating his world at the same speed as the pain in his hands. He tried to move them, but that only made the searing pain worse. As his senses awoke, the first thing to reach past the pain was the awful smell. Dead flesh rotted somewhere nearby and the odor was overwhelming. Bradley realized the smell would be worse if he had both nostrils clear, but something blocked his right nostril.

Bradley's head jerked back into the brace. He blinked rapidly. In front of him on the table was Norman's dead body, but as he'd first seen it. She hadn't cut into his chest yet.

"What the hell?" Bradley murmured.

She appeared from his right where she'd been out of view.

Bradley realized his body was returned to the state it had been when he'd first seen Norman. He looked to where Martin had been placed in the second torture cylinder, but it was nowhere to be seen.

"Exactly, Bradley," she said. "Your reward for a

psychotic life well lived in service to your most depraved desires."

"That means you're trapped in hell too," Bradley said as he smirked.

"Oh Bradley," she giggled. "I'm in heaven. I get to take out my vengeance on you until the next parent who's passed or your own victims get to exact their revenge. There's quite a line, but then we have all eternity don't we? Or maybe, just maybe, this is all in your head and you're just trapped in a hospital somewhere, unable to move, unable to wake up and torturing yourself in your own twisted psyche."

She held up the short handled pruning shears he remembered from the kitchen.

"Doesn't really matter to me what you think. I knew I'd get to use these eventually. Maybe even over and over and over."

"Nooo!" Bradley screamed as she shoved the shears into his abdomen.

As the warm blood flowed from his wound down his leg, he felt his heart slow down with each beat. She reached up and grabbed his left ear, pulling his gaze down to look into her eyes.

"See you again soon," she giggled.

# COMFORT

The smell of fresh wood and graphite shavings always brought a smile to Doctor Howard Penford's face. He wasn't sure if it was the earthiness of the smell or the way it brought him back to his childhood, but it grounded him in ways meditation and medication couldn't. His mind traveled back instantly to carefree and innocent years in elementary school well before reality and the world he lived in crushed his soul.

His reverie was interrupted by a knock on the door. His ten o'clock had arrived.

"Come."

The door opened and Doctor Penford raised his eyebrows at the entrant. Rather than the standard patient attire, Elena Sloane was dressed in a yellow floral print dress and sandals. She still had the standard belt restraint limiting the movement of her arms with her wrists secured in the cuffs on the belt. Still, it was unusual to see a patient in anything but the standard smocks designed for them.

"Interesting attire," Howard remarked. His mind worked at a memory surrounding the dress, but for some reason he couldn't place it. "Special occasion?"

"Someone died," Elena said and smiled innocently.

"Not one of your former patients, I hope," Howard replied straight-faced.

"Agnes from across the hall," one of the guards escorting Elena into the room said. "Kooky broad left her the dress in her will."

"David, isn't it?" Howard said. "We do not use such language here in the facility. Please choose your words more carefully."

"Right," David replied as they locked a chain around the arm of the anchored, padded bench Elena sat down on. "Sorry, this bitch scratched me while we were putting on her belt."

"Patient, she's to be referred to as a patient."

"My apologies, Doctor. It's been a long day. This patient bitch scratched me while we were putting on her belt."

"I see." Howard sighed.

"I don't like restraints," Elena said. "I can't protect myself while I'm wearing them."

David lunged at Elena in an attempt to scare her. She just stared him down, never flinching.

"Whatever," David said. "You behave or one of us will be wiping your ass later."

"Such a flirt," Elena replied, her upper lip curled in disgust.

The two guards left the room, but Howard could see one of them waiting outside the door through the frosted glass, ready to be called in case of trouble. He doubted there would be any, as the patient was well restrained. Howard wrote in his notepad about David needing a talking to before he looked up and smiled at Elena.

"Are you comfortable, Miss Sloane?"

"Yes, Doctor. As comfortable as I can be under the circumstances," Elena replied. She smoothed her flower dress down and rested her palms on her thighs, the limit of her motion with the cuffs on. She shook her head to the right, swinging her long blonde hair behind her shoulder.

"Sorry about that. Your last Doctor felt, uh, threatened." Howard stated and cleared his throat. He flinched a bit as it seemed he may be coming down with something. He took a drink of water and felt a small measure of comfort. It was an odd feeling. He looked at that dress again. Agnes must have been a patient he'd seen, but his memory refused to recall her face.

"I understand," Elena said. She smiled at him. Elena had always admired Doctor Penford's broad shoulders and muscular physique. His thick arms reflected his dedication to his own health and fitness, causing her pulse to quicken. His kind eyes sent a swarm of butterflies chasing around in her stomach while his gentle smile helped put her at ease. There were so many conflicting emotions that Elena hummed a little to herself. She'd never give Doctor Penford any trouble because she preferred his presence to the others.

Unbidden, her mood fouled as the parade of fools she'd had before marched past her mind's eye. The haughty so called Doctor Ben Rothschild and his petulant colleague Doctor Anna Fitzpatrick drew her primary ire. Her mind thrilled a moment at the thought of injecting a little sodium pentathol into their veins so they'd spill their darkest secrets and desires.

"Miss Sloane, are you with me?" Howard asked calmly.

Elena looked up with a gasp, realizing she'd been staring at the floor and grinning madly at her mental exercise.

"Of course, Doctor. My mind just wandered a little thinking about poor Agnes and how at peace she must be now," Elena replied.

"That wasn't by your hand, was it?" Howard asked, calmly writing in the notebook.

"She was never under my care, no. They allowed her to pass in agony," Elena replied sweetly. She took a deep breath as she gazed into his golden brown eyes.

"Well, then. Let's talk about your patients," Howard said with a pleasant smile as he looked down at his notes. "What can you tell me about Henry Tannenbaum?"

"Hank was a delight to all who knew him, a gentleman with a heart of gold. His kindness and generosity were really unrivalled in today's society. A gem of a man if you really must know." Elena smiled at the memory. She turned her hand over and gentle rubbed it against her thigh as she recalled Hank's tender touch.

"I see," Howard replied as he jotted down a few notes. "So, if he was such a wonderful man, why did you kill him?"

"Well, don't you see?" Elena replied, batting her eyelashes. "He was suffering. Anyone as awesome as he was deserved mercy. I gave him that. He even held my hand gently as he passed."

"Yes, your DNA under his fingernails verified you were right there when he passed. The medical records didn't show a terminal illness, however. Mister

Tannenbaum had just had his gall bladder removed.”

"The sepsis had set in. He was in so much pain.” Elena sounded sorrowful.

"Mister Tannenbaum had surgery the previous day with no signs of infection.”

"I do believe his medical records have been falsified by the hospital to protect themselves from liability. I have twenty years experience as an RN. I knew the signs of sepsis and the incredible suffering that can come of it.” Elena smoothed out her dress again as she talked. She had a calm and self assured demeanor. She'd been through these explanations a dozen times already with the others. Elena's nose wrinkled when she reflected on how nasty the others were. They didn't deserve pity or mercy. They were nothing like the calm and gentle Doctor Penford.

"Miss Sloane, you're only thirty-four years old. How can you have twenty years experience?”

"Doctor Penford, as one medical professional to another, you realize we work more than a forty hour week.” Elena smiled sweetly. “Between the extra hours of a residency, extra shifts and additional shifts at another facility, I assure you I gained twenty years worth of experience. It's really just simple math.”

Howard wrote the word 'delusional' down on his notes. He frowned. The simple conclusion lacked the necessary diagnostic underpinnings to it, yet his mind was in a fog. He scribbled 'possibly' in front of it.

"What do you remember about Jenna Pierson?" Howard said with a sigh.

Elena jumped from her seat, but the belt restraint prevented her from getting far. She sat down calmly, took a deep breath and forced a smile.

"Who?" she asked quietly.

"Jenna Pierson, your supervisor in your last position," Howard said as he wrote copious notes on Elena's reaction.

"Oh yes, Nurse Pierson, as the bitch liked to be called."

"You had something against Nurse Pierson?"

Elena looked at the barred window. The sunlight streaming in soothed her rising anger. She breathed in and out a few times.

"Nurse Pierson was troublesome. She was always sticking her nose in where it didn't belong, which is probably why she lost it," Elena said, a darkness creeping into her voice as she recalled her last encounter with the hated supervisor.

"Was? And how do you know she lost her nose?" Howard asked.

"Well..." Elena chuckled as she looked down. "She may still have her nose and she may still 'be,' wherever she is."

"Did you have reason to harm her?" Howard asked and cleared his throat again. The scratchy discomfort was getting harder to ignore.

"She…deserved to be harmed. Such a nasty human being," Elena finished and raised her head to look at Howard with a frown. "Are you feeling okay, Doctor Penford? Something tickling your throat?"

"I'll be fine, thank you," Howard replied and jotted down 'still exhibiting angel of mercy psychosis.'

"I've always liked you, Doctor Penford," Elena said. "It's why your death should be relatively painless."

"You're in no position to do that anymore, Miss Sloane," Howard replied. "I'd like to return to Nurse Pierson."

"Really?" Elena said. "That seems so boring. I thought for sure you'd want to hear about others I've helped recently or perhaps you'd like to hear about future patients of mine!"

"Miss Sloane, I won't indulge your fantasies. You need to come to grips with your presence in this institution and why you're here."

"What institution is that, Doctor Penford?" Elena asked calmly.

"The, um…" Howard frowned in concentration. "State Hospital."

"Which state?"

"This is ridiculous, it's um…" Howard set his pencil down and scratched his head. "Pennsyl… No, Dover? Ahh, Tallahassee!"

"I'm afraid not, Doctor Penford."

"You can dislike being in here all you want, Miss Sloane, but the fact is you're a patient here. Look at your restraints."

Elena slid her hands out of the cuffs and the belt fell onto the bench. She stood up and shrugged.

"What restraints?"

"No," Howard whispered. He got up from his chair and rushed to the door to open it, but it was locked. He pounded on the door frame.

"Guards! Guards! Get in here! She's loose!" Howard shouted and then grabbed his throat.

Elena was at his side in an instant. He didn't remember seeing her move. She just appeared. Howard jumped a half step backward.

"It's all right, Howard," Elena said. "I'll take care of you."

"What's going on," Howard said in a strained voice. "Did you poison my water?"

"Don't you think it's strange I'm in Agnes' dress?" Elena asked as she walked forward slowly like a panther stalking her prey.

Howard shook his head as he stumbled backward. The back of his legs hit the rolling chair and he fell into it. He felt faint and then he went pale.

"Somm… Sommerville?" Howard whispered.

"My most recent patient," Elena said. "She was a bit feisty, I must admit. Obviously, she was very into the gym. Her treatment required special attention and care."

"Agnes," Howard mumbled sadly. Now his mind freely brought her face to mind. They'd shared a few dates together and, though he still carried a torch for her, they'd decided to cool off for a while. Now that he'd found a position at a different hospital, he'd hoped to rekindle their romance. No professional barriers if they didn't work at the same facility anymore.

"This was her favorite dress, wasn't it Doctor Penford? The one you bought for her just six months ago."

"No, it's… how could you know that?" Howard looked up in awe at Elena.

"Did you know I can enter the minds of my patients, Doctor Penford? It's a thrilling experience. I can tell immediately what kind of setting they'd be most comfortable in for their transition, what they'd like for their final meal and who they'd like to have at their side. While I couldn't bring Agnes to mind for you, I decided wearing her dress would do just as well. Even better, since it's me in it!"

"You can't do that." Howard shook his head. His throat hurt so badly. He could still breathe fine, but it felt like he had a tube stuck into his throat. He tried to raise his hands to his throat, but found they were strapped to his chair. His chair stretched out below him, transforming into a hospital bed. His wrists were stuck in a belt restraint like Elena had been wearing. His feet similarly restrained. "This isn't possible!"

"I thought you'd like to know that I've decided Doctor Rothschild and Doctor Fitzpatrick will face a less pleasant end. Such nasty beasts!" Elena screwed her face up in rage and pounded on bed rails. Then she looked with horror at Howard. "Oh, I'm so sorry. Whenever I think about them, I just get so angry. They put me in solitary, strapped to a bed. For weeks, I endured David and his grubby mitts pawing at my flesh like some kind of animal. You know, I thought I could handle his molestations until he climbed on top of me the second week and penetrated me. That was the last straw. That's when I planned my escape. After two more weeks of rapes, assault, and sodomy, I was let out of solitary. I told Agnes and she advocated for me. She's why I was able to get out. During the transfer to the new facility, I escaped during a potty break and fled into the woods."

"Miss Sloane, I'm sorry that happened to you. But

you have to turn yourself in! You're not well," David's throat hurt whether he talked or not. He realized it wasn't a symptom of speaking, but of something else. He imagined a tube was down his throat. A ventilator most likely, but how had he come to be in a hospital he didn't know.

"Barbados," Elena replied to his thoughts. "You went on vacation in Barbados. I followed you here after I relieved Miss Sommerville of her earthly burden. She was very sweet. You two really should've stayed together. You could've known real happiness together. You could've left this mortal coil together." Elena trailed off with the last thought. "I'm not going to do that for Rothschild and Fitzpatrick! They'll die alone in agony!"

"What happened to Agnes?" Howard asked. Tears fell from his eyes.

"Oh, I shouldn't have told you about her," Elena said softly as she wiped away his tears. "I wanted this passage to be gentler for you."

Elena stood up and walked to the foot of the bed. As she did so, the room slowly changed and Howard recognized the interior of a hospital room, having been in several before on volunteer rotations. The window was cracked slightly, letting in a soft ocean breeze. But was this the real room or just what Elena wanted him to see?

Elena turned to him and smiled.

"You picked the location," she said and she turned back to the window, looking out. "Arranging your accident on the Jet Ski was fairly simple, ensuring you'd be taken to this facility. You'd be surprised at the criminal element you can find anywhere that will do your bidding for the right price. I'd only just started my shift when you came in. Surgery first, to relieve the pressure on your brain and then they put you in here. You will, of course, have died from complications after your accident. Don't think you lot haven't taught me to cover my tracks better, so something good came from my time in hell."

"I don't remember..." Howard said groggily.

"Oh, I know. Head trauma like that will give you all sorts of memory issues. Let's say I botch this procedure and you survive. Even if you recall anything of our time together, it will be written off as a hallucination. No one will believe you. It's really quite a thrilling situation, isn't it?"

"Agnes..." Howard struggled to keep his eyes open. "What happened to Agnes?"

"All right, if you must know. I always did have a soft spot for you." Elena sighed and walked back to his bedside. She sat down and held his hand. "I know you cared for her, so I didn't want her to suffer. She was kind to me as well, so it was only right to be kind in return."

"What did you do?"

"Agnes was visiting her parents and she was overcome by carbon monoxide one night in her bedroom while she was sleeping. My visit to her mind was more like a dream. I thanked her for her kindness." Elena looked off into the distance. "Even in the dream she was kind to me. Oh, you two should've stayed together! How romantic would it have been for you to both wander off into the sky together, alone amongst the stars?"

Howard tried to scratch her hand with his thumb. Elena looked down and smiled.

"I told you I'd learned," Elena responded and held up her hands which were covered by dark blue nitrile gloves. "Two layers. It's amazing what going over all my comforting events did for my future planning. Thank you for that."

"Please, I don't want to die," Howard whispered.

"Everyone dies, Doctor Penford," Elena said. "Are you in pain?"

Howard realized he wasn't in pain and a sort of calm took over him. He wondered if Elena's other patients had felt the same at the end and then thought maybe it wasn't such a bad thing.

# COLLAPSE

The body slid to a dull wet thud on the floor. While the connection with the concrete may have fractured the skull in some way, the injury didn't matter in the end. The blonde woman's eyes fluttered as she gasped her last breath, her face a contorted mass of bubbling purple splotches. Finally, she stopped shuddering as her last breathe left her body and she fixed him with her dying gaze, her blue irises surrounded by the hemorrhaging blood vessels in the white of her eyes. One of the eyeballs popped open, spewing the gooey, bloodied aqueous humor from her ruptured eye socket.

Her lone observer turned and retched on the lab floor. He grabbed the counter of the silver and white cabinet for support as he just let go all over the tile beneath his feet.

"Are you all right, Will?" a woman's voice said over the speakers hidden in the ceiling.

"Yeah," Will Traynor said as he grabbed a towel from the dispenser and wiped his mouth. "Can you just…"

He waved his hand in the dead woman's direction behind a thick pane of glass.

"Initiating decontamination protocol seven," the woman replied and the room with the corpse lit up with a blue and white flame. Steel safety doors lowered and blocked the scene from Will's view as he took a few steps to the right out of the puddle of lunch.

Will ran some water in the sink and splashed the cold water on his face. He grabbed another towel, wet it and cleaned off his shoes.

"Will, I'm sorry for your loss." The woman's voice came over the speakers low and quiet.

"Don't worry about it, Katarina. We've all lost someone," Will said and took a deep breath. "I knew this was coming when we brought her here two days ago. None of the interventions worked as I'd anticipated and feared."

Will picked up a coffee cup from the counter by the sink and threw it with all his might at the steel safety door and screamed. He picked up a metal chair and threw it as well. It clanged off the safety door and landed somewhere near his vomit. He put his hands on his knees and took several deep breaths. He closed his eyes and slowed his breathing until it was controlled and calm returned. He stood up slowly and walked to the door behind him.

"Let's get back at it, Katarina," Will said as he pushed the door open and walked to the stairwell. Tears streamed down his face. He let them flow as he worked on his breathing. He took the steps two at a time and ascended the two floors to the ground floor. Katarina, a redheaded woman roughly in her thirties, Will had never asked, waited there for him in a lab coat with a face full of sympathy. She'd lost her husband and daughter just a week ago. Her green eyes twinkled with tears.

"We'll try batch 57," Will said, his voice cracking, but Katarina just ran to him and hugged him, crying tears she'd been holding back for a week. He'd never seen her cry. She'd just had a stiff upper lip for the last week, unable to see her family in quarantine before they'd died. She couldn't hold it back any longer. Her compassion broke the dam Will had been building to hold his own emotions in check until they could be processed later. He joined her tears and hugged her with all his might. They shared a horrible life experience, like so many had already.

An older man's voice crackled to life over the speakers.

"Outpost 40? Are you there?"

Katarina stood up, huffed a breath out and sniffled. She wiped her tears away and faced the ceiling.

"This is Outpost 40," Katarina replied. "Is that you, General?"

"You're it," the voice huffed. The strain was evident. "I'm the last one at 23." The man's voice cracked and he devolved into a fit of coughing.

"What?" Will asked.

"Everyone's gone," the man said. "I just watched Doctor Tripp explode in the control room, bathing everything in bloody mucus. I'm not far behind, perhaps an hour or two. God, the pain is unbearable!"

In his mind's eye, Will could see the good General fighting the virus with all his might and losing miserably.

"I didn't know," Will said.

"I've uploaded the last of the data to the central system, but Will," the General said. "There's hardly anyone left. I can't reach Washington, state or local officials. Nobody."

"Katarina and I don't even have a fever," Will replied.

"You've both got some kind of immunity," the General said. "There's no way with the runaway infection rate you weren't exposed like the rest of us. Check your own antibodies. For the ones you might be able to save. Maybe a vaccine, maybe a cure. Not sure what humanity has left…"

The General coughed violently and the line went silent.

"We'd been working on Marla all night," Katarina said. "I never checked the feeds."

"Let's get up to control. See if there's anything left."

They walked down the hallway to another stairwell and walked quietly up the stairs. Between his wife's excruciating death a moment ago and the news from the General just now, Will was pretty sure he was in shock. It was the only way to explain how he wasn't breaking down right now.

Minutes later, they entered the control room. Huge screens hung on the walls, ten feet high and fifteen across. The room seemed cavernous with just the two of them. They walked to the control systems in the center and adjusted the feeds on each of the screens. A few of the feeds just showed static, indicating they'd gone completely offline. They cycled through until they found several static camera shots. The unmanned camera angles revealed a city of death, silence and little movement. Outside of a stray bird or in the case of Chicago, a brisk wind that shuffled debris around, nothing moved.

The computer to the left of Katarina beeped and

they both jumped. Katarina unlocked the screen and manipulated the system until she'd opened a message. She read the screen and her face went white.

"Will, it's from Dr. Samuels," she said and nearly collapsed in the chair behind her.

Will's face contorted in rage.

"Everything's gone and now he shows up?"

"He's sending a helicopter for us," Katarina said.

"So we can crash when the pilot dies?" Will picked up a clipboard and flung it across the room.

Katarina rolled back to the computer and continued reading.

"It's a drone," Katarina said. She squinted her eyes shut. "Where the hell has he been the last two months?"

"We'll ask him when we see him," Will said. "If I die while killing him, it will be worth it."

A whirring hum sounded above their heads and Will looked at Katarina.

"You'll have competition," Katarina said with a scowl. She got up and walked to the exit. Will followed close behind.

The drone sat hovering just a few inches off the ground, buoyed by huge rotors underneath. A ladder on the left led a few steps up to a cabin door. Katarina was first up the ladder and Will closed the door after them.

They sat in the only two seats in the vehicle. There were no visible controls; just a set of cameras facing them. The cabin was nearly silent. They could barely detect a whisper of the four sets of massive whirring fans below them.

"Doctors Traynor and Kalinskiya confirmed aboard. Please buckle your seatbelts as we prepare to ascend," a kind but clearly robotic voice told them. Will and Katarina buckled their seatbelts; the whirring sound increased slightly and they rose into the air smoothly.

Will looked out the window and saw the rain forest pass quickly beneath them and slowly change to a dark green patch below them. Judging from their northern trajectory, they were either going to Bogota, somewhere in Venezuela or perhaps out into the gulf. The Peruvian border disappeared behind them quickly.

"What happens next?" Katarina asked, her Russian accent coming through as her voice shook. Will looked at her and the adrenaline that got her on board the helicopter was clearly fading. She was pale. Will reached under him and found drawers filled with drinks and salty snacks. He opened a bottle of water and handed it to her.

"For now, you take a drink. I think perhaps we'll both grab a snack before we rest our eyes for a few minutes or hours," Will said as she took the bottle and gulped it down. Will retrieved some trail mix packages and opened them, handing one to Katarina.

"Perhaps we should've eaten before we left." Katarina chuckled nervously.

"I think we'll be all right," Will replied and smiled. "Marcus is known for his appetite; I'm certain he'll have a healthy supply of food wherever he's been hiding. Assuming he doesn't kill us on the way to see him, that is."

"I've never known Doctor Samuels to be a violent man," Katarina said. She opened the drawer beneath her own seat and rifled through it, coming up with a small bottle of vodka. "Pretty elaborate way of doing away with us. He could have just crashed the drone into the complex."

"I'm interested to know how he knew where we even were," Will said. He munched on a handful of nuts and dried fruit. "He disappeared before there was even an access list he could haughtily refuse to be on."

"It's strange," Katarina agreed. "Why disappear before the greatest logistical and scientific puzzle the human race has ever faced? He'd be in nirvana fighting this, even from a small eccentric lab high up in the Andes."

"Maybe that's where we're heading," Will laughed.

"Then we would've headed south or at least east," Katarina replied. She unscrewed the lid from the vodka and took a swig. She offered it to Will.

"I'm more of a whiskey man," Will said as he shook his head.

"You're not missing much," Katarina grimaced. "This clearly wasn't brewed in Russia. Ah well, beggars cannot choose."

She downed the rest of the tiny bottle and Will chuckled.

"Beggars can't be choosers," he said as he pulled up a tiny bottle of whiskey.

"If we're the last two people on earth and you die first," Katarina winked. "The history books will reflect it my way."

Hours later, Will awoke with a start as he noticed a change in the sound of the fans below. He felt the vehicle slightly incline forward as they dropped down toward what he thought was probably the coast of Venezuela. Katarina was already awake and pointed out the window.

"Caracas," she noted. "But our trajectory is taking us out toward the ocean. Perhaps he's on a ship?"

"Easier to hide in the great wide open of the world's oceans." Will nodded. "With enough supplies, you can be out on the water for months, even years if you have a renewable fuel source. Maybe he's sitting out the pandemic there."

"We'll have to go through some kind of decontamination when we arrive then. He wouldn't allow us to infect his safe haven."

"He abandoned humanity in their hour of need. An infection is the least of his worries." Will looked down at Caracas, but they were still too high up to see anything of note except a general lack of any movement.

"Why contact us at all?" Katarina looked at Will. "What does he have to gain at this point?"

Will just shook his head and shrugged. The adrenaline from his wife's death had worn off and he felt a weariness fall upon him. He sat back in the seat and stared ahead, trying to gather the energy for the confrontation with his former mentor.

As the coast disappeared behind them, the drone continued to descend until a fairly large yacht on the surface of the water below began to emerge.

"It's anchored with a skiff tied to the side in the water," Katrina noted as she looked down. Will nodded and took a deep breath. Katrina stuffed a few snacks in her pocket from the drone drawer and grabbed a bottle of water. She held the bottle of water up to Will. "We don't know what the situation is down there."

Will blinked, took another breath and nodded. He

rifled through his drawer and got supplies as well. His eyes landed on the flare gun by the console of the drone. He put it in his pocket with two flare cartridges.

The drone landed and the doors automatically opened. They cautiously exited the craft, but there was no ambush. In fact, there was no one on the deck at all or within sight. They made their way slowly from the landing pad on the bow of the vessel to the top of three decks. Katrina noticed the bridge of the ship appeared to be abandoned. She opened the door and was greeted by the expired corpse of someone who had succumbed to the virus. She closed the door quickly and wretched over the side of the yacht, her snack from the helicopter leaving her quicker than it had been consumed. Through the closed door, Will looked at what he could recognize on the bridge console. It appeared they were anchored and the engines did not appear to be running at all.

"I wonder if there's anyone alive on this ship," Katrina managed and then took a quick gulp from her water bottle. She swished the water around and spit it out over the side.

"Well, there are at least two more decks and likely another below the water line. Let's go exploring," Will replied. They looked in the room behind the bridge and found no one there.

As they descended the ship, they located two

more victims of the plague and no one alive until they reached the third deck down, the one just above the water. As Katrina opened the doors, they heard a strained voice welcome them.

"Welcome Doctor Traynor and Doctor Kalinskiya, we've been expecting you," a voice called from the darkness of the huge cabin. As they stepped inside, lights came on revealing a large scientific bay with a section at the rear partitioned off by glass. Dr. Marcus Samuels sat in a chair facing them. He looked like he was in the final stages of the infection himself, although his skin was a much darker purple than anything they'd seen before, almost black.

"We?" Katrina said as she glanced around the room quickly.

Dr. Samuels rose from the chair and moved a few stilted steps forward. He placed a slick, mottled hand upon the glass, opened his milky white eyes and curved his face in an unnatural smile. Thick, purple goo dripped a thin, lazy line from his opened mouth down his soiled lab coat, disappearing into the stained cloth.

"Dr. Samuels has been kind enough to lend me his body to communicate more effectively with you," his stilted voice pronounced. "Well, it wasn't really his choice."

Katrina and Will glanced at each other just for a

moment and then returned their gaze to Dr. Samuels. Will frowned. At this stage in the infection, speech would be extremely difficult if not impossible. While Dr. Samuels' speech was clearly not normal, it was much clearer than it should be.

"Who are you if you're not Dr. Samuels?" Katrina asked.

Dr. Samuels cocked his head to the left for a moment and then straightened back up.

"I don't have a name, per se. I've been here since the world was formed. Well before your quaint superstitions ever formed. You may call me Earth or Marcus as you see fit. We've been together so long now, it seems like we're almost one," Dr. Samuels gave a brief giggle.

"We've know him a long time now. How long have you known him?" Will asked.

"I selected you for the program, which is why you were both hired."

"We haven't worked together until this virus and you left before we were assigned to Outpost 40," Katrina scoffed. "We weren't born yesterday."

"I didn't select you to work on the virus," Dr. Samuels said. A pool of fluid was gathering near his left shoe, drawing Will's attention to his feet. Will couldn't escape the feeling he was talking to a dead man.

"What then? The chickenshit program? Is that why you disappeared when this virus arose?" Will was going to get his attacks in even if it was only to a man seconds from death.

"You are both just perfect for each other," Dr. Samuels said.

"What?" Katrina laughed.

"I selected you both for the Survival Program," Dr. Samuels said. "If you recall, you were both vaccinated before your last assignments."

"Kenya," Will said. "Why?"

"I was Panama," Katrina said. "What did you do to us?"

"You were selected to survive along with nearly one hundred thousand others," Dr. Samuels said.

"Vaccinated against what exactly," Will asked. His hand grasped the flare gun tightly in his pocket.

"What you call Arganus Syndrome." Dr. Samuels cocked his head to the left again. "I designed the virus to reset the planet."

Will pulled the flare gun out of his pocket, loaded the cartridge and shot it at the glass barrier. It shattered on impact, sending Dr. Samuels backward onto his back. As they watched, crab like appendages sprouted from his sides, easily bursting through the flimsy lab coat. The limbs looked like they were made of human bones, sinew and flesh. His regular arms and legs had disappeared. What was Dr. Samuels flipped onto its' spindly legs. Dr. Samuels head rose up on a long thin stalk of a neck and glared at them.

"You cannot harm me, humans. I inhabit this flesh at my whim only to communicate. The earth has enacted its judgment!"

Will put another flare cartridge in the gun and fired at the abomination moving crazily on the slippery floor. The flare lit up the former Dr. Samuels and burned brightly. The sickening scream that erupted from the creature forced Will and Katrina to slap their hands over their ears as they ran from the room.

Smoke billowed from the lower deck and they ran to the front of the ship to escape it. They climbed onto the landing pad and moved toward the drone.

"Will and Katrina," a voice called to them in a thick, moist voice from above. They turned to the bridge and saw the remains of the ship's captain next to the bridge staring at them from eyeballs broken and oozing from their sockets. "Tell your fellow humans to respect the earth or they'll be wiped from the face of the planet forever. I won't be so selective next time."

# DYSMORPHIA

gent Kellogg, please have a seat," the bald man with the glasses said as Martin entered the room. Martin walked to the single chair at the end of a large ten by six foot table and took a seat. Across from him sat three men six feet away, two in suits and the bald man in a white doctor's smock.

Martin assessed the men who had called him in to review the details of this project gone horribly wrong. The bald man with glasses presented as a doctor or scientist of some kind, perhaps in charge or perhaps just the one guiding the review. To the doctor's left sat a man with dark hair like Martin's own, but closer shaven on the sides. Perhaps the man had a military background or just liked to think he did. The suit he wore seemed to be strained, trying to contain the bulk of muscles this man enjoyed showing off. He sat at near attention and Martin could feel the tension in the man's grey eyes as he stared at Martin, a slight frown on his face. Possibly didn't approve of Martin or perhaps the entire project, Martin wasn't sure. Was he trying to project anger or intimidation? He didn't look happy, regardless.

The man to the doctor's right seemed calm. Martin decided it was more than likely this was the money man, the one in charge of procuring funds and getting the green light for the kinds of Black Ops projects Martin worked on. His nails were neatly manicured, his suit fit like a glove, obviously tailored. Not a hair out of place, even his eyebrows appeared meticulously groomed.

Martin knew none of their names and had never seen them before today.

"Agent Kellogg," the doctor said as he leafed through a plain manila folder in front of him. "It says here you've been with the Altered Project from day one."

"I was involved with the dispersal of the chemical or biological agent inside Aaron Platt's room, yes. However, I was not involved in the project before that day. None of the planning or organization; I'm just the agent in the field."

"The Agent in Charge," the military man said with a gruff voice. Martin mused it was gruff because he was always yelling.

"In charge of the field operations, yes, but not the

project. I assume that's you guys?"

The doctor went to answer, but the money man put his hand on his arm and the doctor fell silent.

"We'll ask the questions, Agent Kellogg," the money man said in a quiet voice that caused the other two men to take a deep breath. Oh yeah, money man was definitely in charge.

"Of course," Martin nodded.

"What do you know of Mister Platt?" the doctor said and smiled. Obviously, he was trying to regain control of the interview, trying to put Martin at ease.

"I had full access to his file," Martin replied. "Mister Platt is a financial analyst with a psychiatric history of body dysmorphia. Perfect subject to experiment on with some kind of appearance changing drug, I believe."

"That wasn't in the file," the doctor said plainly.

"There was some kind of warning label on the containers we installed in his air vents. I believe one of the technicians assisting me said something about not spilling it on myself or my physical appearance might uncontrollably change. Perhaps he was just trying to scare me, but I certainly didn't spill. From the way the experiment progressed, I contend his explanation was pretty accurate."

"Probably Stiles," the doctor said to the military

man.

"I'll have him terminated," the military man replied.

Martin shuddered. Stiles, whoever he was, wasn't about to lose his job. He was about to lose his life. Black Ops was dangerous that way.

"The compound alone could not create that effect," the doctor said. "You recall switching out his psychotics?"

"I made the required replacements of his maintenance drugs. They were switched back after phase one completed, as is standard procedure. Was that a mistake?" Martin wondered aloud. He hadn't received alternate instructions beyond the initial briefing, so he wasn't sure if something had gone wrong with that phase.

"That is how it was supposed to transpire," the doctor replied. Martin nodded in relief. Mistakes were a certain path to termination as well.

"You were outside his psychiatrist's office on day thirteen, correct?" The doctor asked.

"I did submit a report as such," Martin replied. "Are you questioning the report?"

"Agent Kellogg, just answer the questions please," money man said quickly.

"Yes sir," Martin replied.

"Where were you when the incident took place?" The doctor asked.

"Two doors down sitting on a waiting room bench," Martin leaned forward, agitated by the second degree he was getting. "As I noted in the report."

"Did you hear what transpired in," the doctor looked at his notes, "Doctor Felix's office?"

"Not until the screaming started," Martin said. "It took me less than fifteen seconds to reach the door. It was locked. The screaming stopped before I could shoot the lock and get the door open. I don't recall hearing anything intelligible."

"You couldn't open the door silently?" The military man asked accusingly.

"Not quickly," Martin replied without hesitation. "Lock picking takes some concentration and some time, especially if it wasn't something I was ready to do. Shooting the lock was faster by a minimum of 120 seconds, probably more like five minutes."

"Still, you could've tried," the military man pressed.

"To what end?" Martin asked. "I needed to get in to assess the situation. My briefings didn't say anything about being prepared for an attack at this phase. Perhaps the briefing was faulty. I'm in charge of executing the operation as written, not planning it myself.”

The military man sat back in his leather seat, his face a little redder now. Martin guessed he'd been in charge of the threat assessment and planning. This looked bad for him which happily wasn't Martin's problem.

"What happened when you opened the door?" The doctor returned the interview to the facts, for which Martin was grateful. He wasn't looking to have a pissing match with the military man; the guy was probably there to try to get him off balance. He took a breath to center himself.

"Mister Platt or what I thought was Mister Platt threw Doctor Felix's severed head at me."

"How did you know it was Doctor Felix's head?" the doctor asked.

"Well, it was a severed head. I didn't learn it was Doctor Felix's until afterward," Martin said.

"Why didn't you shoot Mister Platt then?" the military man asked.

"Operation objective forbid it," Martin said looking at the military man incredulously. "I assumed you wrote the rules of engagement."

"You were allowed to wound him," the military man said sternly.

"I was too busy dodging a bloody head to get a

non-lethal bead on Mister Platt. That split second was all Mister Platt needed to jump out the window."

"That is where you failed," the military man said. "You should've had agents outside the window to intercept him should he try to escape."

The military man sat back and folded his arms with satisfaction.

"My team was covering the exits a normal human being would use," Martin said. "Doors, stairwells, fire escapes. We were on the fourth floor. There was nothing in the briefing or file about Mister Platt being an enhanced individual."

The doctor looked down for just a moment, but that was enough to let Martin know this part of the project was the doctor's screw-up.

"Look, I'm not a scientist, but it's pretty obvious someone gave him the wrong dose, the wrong drug or didn't evaluate their target properly before choosing him for the experiment," Martin said hotly.

The doctor tensed and nearly stood up, but the money man pressed his hand firmly on the doctor's forearm.

"There's no reason to be making accusations," the money man said firmly.

"Isn't there?" Martin replied. "You think this is the first operation I've been on where the higher ups screwed up and then tried to find a scapegoat? Hardly. My value to this organization is because I'm the one who doesn't screw up. Blame this mess on Stiles if you must; he's obviously expendable."

The three men stared daggers at Martin. He just sat back calmly in his chair and raised his eyebrows. Money man smiled, turned to the doctor and said "Continue."

"Why didn't you fire at Mister Platt once he exited the window?" the military man asked with a sigh.

"He wasn't there," Martin said.

"What do you mean he wasn't there?" The doctor asked.

"It's in the report," Martin said. "No one below, no one above, and no one to either side. I contacted my team immediately to be vigilant at the exits even though I was relatively sure Mister Platt wouldn't be using any of them."

"We reviewed the statements in the report," the doctor said. "You state there was damage below the window and along the wall all the way down as if someone had climbed down that way."

"I watched what I believed to be Mister Platt at the time doing damage to the side of the building evidenced by bits of plaster and brick falling from the outer wall," Martin said. "I heard something scrambling along the wall even though nothing was visible. I heard it land on the ground and then footsteps as it ran away, fading into the distance. Never saw anything to shoot at and it was broad daylight."

"That's impossible," the military man said.

"We don't have any data indicating that level of physical change is possible in a human being," the doctor continued.

"Now you do," Martin replied. "I suspect you're not completely surprised. You clearly anticipated he would change his physical appearance based on the technician's slip up. I'm thinking the only thing you didn't count on was his ability to control it so fast. Or perhaps he was controlling it subconsciously. Fight or flight response of a chameleon."

The men sat there for a few seconds staring at each other. Martin smiled. His suspicions were all conjecture based on observation, but he knew they were right. The doctor looked down at his notes again.

"You didn't find the weapon that was used on Doctor Felix," the doctor said.

"That was strange," Martin acknowledged. "Doctor Felix's body had been shredded and torn apart in a matter of maybe two minutes. I'll be honest; I don't know what weapon could do something like that. Not a conventional weapon anyway."

"What are you implying?" the money man said and sat forward in his chair. Martin nodded and smiled. Yeah, this was the big money moment for him. Something he could sell to the higher ups for additional research, more experiments. Martin could just imagine the prospect of having this kind of technology for covert operations worldwide.

"You did something to Mister Platt that didn't stop at his physical appearance," Martin said. "Somehow, you gave him the ability to alter or manipulate his entire body, changing it into a weapon. Hardened skin to bludgeon, extended nails or even bone manipulated in such a way as to puncture, cut, slice, whatever."

"You surmised this right then?" the doctor asked.

"I surmised something strange was going on when I wandered back out of Doctor Felix's office through bits of Doctor Felix, his entrails splashed over the desk. He looked like he'd been attacked by a chainsaw, bone saw and food processor."

"A bit dramatic," the military man said. "I've seen the same thing on the battlefield."

"Yeah, but that's usually the result of an IED or point blank automatic weapon fire," Martin replied. "How could a normal human being do that to another human being with no explosives and no discernible weapons of any kind?"

"Fascinating," the money man said.

"Is this why you increased the firepower for the confrontation at Mister Platt's apartment?" the doctor asked.

"And the technology," Martin replied. "I figured if he could change his physical appearance, it was at least possible he hadn't figured out how to mask his heat signature. Still required to bring him in alive per the engagement rules."

Martin glanced at the military man who nervously cleared his throat.

"So," Martin continued. "Nothing lethal. Heat seeking tranquilizer darts in all the weapons. Two men on the roof to cover the windows leading from Mister Platt's apartment."

"I can't see how he could escape that kind of dragnet," the military man said. "Yet, he escaped?"

"The two men on the roof were slaughtered first. Let's assume Mister Platt didn't have knowledge of weaponry, so there's no way he could have known we were attempting to deploy non-lethal methods to bring him in."

"They alerted command they were under attack?" The military man sat forward, arms resting on the table. This was clearly his area of expertise. Martin could just imagine his pulse racing with excitement.

"They were dead before they could make a sound," Martin said. "Somehow, Mister Platt had entered the building undetected, left the men guarding the entrances alone, and gone to the roof to methodically remove the threat."

"There was nothing in his profile suggesting skills of any sort," the doctor said.

"Well, this is where things start to get really strange. Agent Bryant arrived at the location as backup to the team, part of a ten-man crew sent by you folks."

The three sat back and looked at each other nervously.

"That wasn't in the report," the doctor said while reexamining the paperwork in front of him.

"I didn't name every member of the team," Martin replied. "Agent Bryant was sent by you, so I assumed you had a list of the team members you sent."

"Nine," the military man said. "We sent a nine member team. Agent Bryant wasn't on the team. He couldn't have been."

"Why was that exactly?" Martin asked.

"Agent, we ask—" the money man began, but the military man waved him off.

"He died at another site thirty minutes prior to your operation," the military man said.

"So, Mister Platt had disguised himself as Agent Bryant," Martin said. "I'd go so far as to surmise, Mister Platt was the one who ended Agent Bryant's life."

"Immaterial," the military man said.

"Is it?" Martin responded. "Did Agent Bryant have knowledge of our operation? Could he have leaked that information, willingly or not?"

"His wounds were not consistent with torture," the doctor said. "There is evidence he may have been restrained prior to his death, but any decent agent can resist torture and there's no reason to suspect he experienced any long period of torture."

"So, willingly then," Martin said.

This time, money man stood up and slapped his hands down on the table.

"I will not have you disrespect the memory of a top agent like this!"

"I'm certain the good doctor here is mistaken and torture or something else forced the information from Agent Bryant," Martin said coolly. "I'm not naïve. Standard operating procedure for taking a civilian in to never be seen again is to lay a cover story about his disappearance and, if necessary, elimination of people he is in contact with to maintain the cover story. My guess, based on the callous disregard for anyone's well being at Mister Platt's apartment building is he stumbled upon this organization eliminating someone with a very personal connection to Mister Platt."

"If you're suggesting we're responsible," the money man began.

"I watched six of my men surround Mister Platt," Martin said, rising from his chair as his own anger grew. "They were literally torn in half simultaneously while Mister Platt disappeared from view! You've seen the footage as well as I have! Had you had the balls to communicate the danger my team faced, they may be alive today and Mister Platt may not be on the loose!"

"We have footage from his lover's apartment— Agent Bryant said nothing!" The money man was standing as well.

"What happened to Agent Bryant?" Martin said calmly as he sat down.

"It's not your place to ask!" the money man shouted again.

"If we're to get to the bottom of how Mister Platt operates, what abilities he has gained, we need to be more collaborative," the doctor said. "Show the footage from Daria Tannen's home, Agent Bryant's last minute alive."

On the wall to Martin's left, a screen built into the wall jumped to life. A video showing a time code popped up. Agent Bryant, in full tactical gear, raised his right hand with a revolver in it, but the man in front of him waved his arm and something unseen on the footage sliced Agent Bryant's hand off at the wrist. The gun fell to the ground and fired harmlessly into a wall.

The figure assumed to be Mister Platt raised his other arm and what can only be described as shards of razor sharp bone erupted from his fingers, impaled Agent Bryant through the shoulders and thighs and pushed him against the wall. This rendered Agent Bryant immobile for all intents and purposes.

As Agent Bryant struggled against the wall, Mister Platt walked closer until he was inches from Agent Bryant's face. A shard drove into Agent Bryant's nostril and exited through to the wall behind him, immobilizing his skull. Another shard drove through his closed right eye, which erupted in vitreous fluid and blood that dripped down Agent Bryant's face as he screamed helplessly.

The two remained locked in that position for nearly thirty seconds until the bone shards withdrew from Agent Bryant's skull and his head flopped forward. The rest of the bone shards impaling Agent Bryant retracted back into Mister Platt and the operative's limp body fell to the floor.

Back in the interview room, the military man looked a bit green while the doctor and money man appeared nonplussed.

"You see," the money man said smugly. "Bryant never said a word."

"And Platt never asked a question," Martin replied. "What was going on with the shard through the eye? Thirty seconds is a long time."

"Agent Bryant was lobotomized," the doctor replied. "Clearly, it took some time to accomplish."

"Why not just kill him?" Martin leaned forward on the table and folded his hands together. "You don't find that odd? You've seen the footage from his apartment. It took him no time, literally, to slice six men in half. I contend he absorbed Agent Bryant's memories somehow, read his mind or ingested it or something."

"Preposterous!" The military man scoffed. "There's nothing to suggest anything of the sort!"

The doctor simply tapped his pen on the table and looked lost in thought. The money man was curiously silent on the matter. The military man looked at his associates and his eyes got wide.

"You can't be serious?" he said and his jaw dropped open.

"Possible side effect," the doctor murmured. He turned to the money man. "The catalyst worked much faster than anticipated."

"So, to sum up," Martin replied. "You badly ran an

operation with poor communication, created a super human assassin you have no control over and you're desperate to find someone to be your scapegoat. Sound about right?"

"Your impertinence will be the end of your career," the money man said plainly.

Martin placed his hands in his lap.

"You're assuming there is a career to save," Martin said. "Just as you've been fools to assume I'm really Martin Kellogg."

The three men gasped as bone shards penetrated their abdomens and ran through them, severing their spinal columns and pushed through the backs of the leather chairs. Blood trickled onto the floor beneath the three chairs. As the men shuddered with a look of shock on their faces, the daggers of bone reentered their bodies just below the neck, traveled up through the spinal cords into their brains and began absorbing the information trapped in the paralyzed men's minds.

"It's really too bad," Aaron said as his face transformed to his own features again. "Had you but approached me, I might have been an ally, cooperative, even an asset. But you decided to slaughter Daria and, as I came to understand it, several members of my immediate family. When you think about it, this was the only real logical outcome, don't you agree?"

The shards of bone withdrew from the men and they all collapsed onto the ground.

Aaron stood up and walked over to the door.

"I won't kill you immediately. You'll die soon enough of your wounds; my guess is you'll slowly suffocate over the next few minutes before anyone can get you to any kind of medical triage for treatment. I've left you alive to consider the consequences you've suffered for the sins you've committed. I'll be visiting your colleagues soon enough based on the information I've gleaned from your troubling minds. It's time for this Black Ops travesty to end."

The surveillance devices in the room recorded Aaron Platt opening the door and then disappearing from view. The offices in the covert facility ran thick with blood that night as everyone in the building was slaughtered by an unseen assailant.

# BURDEN OF GUILT

He's in my sights. I can take the shot," Zeus said as he stared without blinking through the scope.

"Do it. Don't think about it, just do it," Jeffrey replied watching his friend with a buzz cut on the ground from just a few paces back. He ran his fingers through his own darks locks and sniffed nervously.

Zeus lay prone on the ground, the sniper rifle in his hands jutting out just over the edge of the inclined cliff. Far below, several klicks away, a well muscled man with thinning gray hair waited for his wife to emerge from their two-story house. Flashes of the man, twenty years younger, coming at Zeus with both fists, a belt and then a chunk of PVC pipe popped into Zeus' mind. He blinked rapidly and retrained his sights on the man. A woman with a noticeable bulge in her belly emerged and smiled at the man.

"I might hit her instead," Zeus said as he

continued holding his rifle steady.

"Bullshit. Eight years as a decorated sniper, how could you miss?" Jeffrey scoffed.

"One brain shot and she'd have his cerebellum splattered all over her. She'd never recover," Zeus replied.

"Like mom never recovered? You remember what he did to mom? He'll never stop."

"You don't understand," Zeus said. His trigger finger trembled against the small piece of carbon steel separating the man below from life or death.

"I was there, Zeus!" Jeffrey yelled. "I'm just as much a victim as you are! I'd switch places with you, but you know I can't. Just pull the damn trigger. Don't let another child become his next victim."

Zeus watch the pair get into the car. He kept his sights trained on the man even as he pulled out of the driveway and drove down the road. One shot through the windshield would end it all. Moments later, the car turned away from him. The shot was gone.

Zeus laid the weapon on the ground next to him and stood up. He turned to face Jeffrey, who glared at him with a hatred that nearly matched what Zeus felt for the man in the canyon below.

"Four tours and you've calmly executed men who've done less," Jeffrey spewed with all the venom he could. "You're pathetic."

"Yeah," Zeus said quietly as he picked up the rifle, unloaded the cartridge and walked by Jeffrey toward the car. "I am."

"Why did we even come up here?" Jeffrey continued as he followed Zeus through the low, dry brush to the road where the car was parked on the shoulder. "You said you'd had enough. The nightmares… well, I guess they weren't too much after all."

Zeus turned and glared at Jeffrey.

"I don't know why I can't kill him, okay?"

"So that's it? You're just going to be a chickenshit while he beats more children in the privacy of his own home? Who knows, maybe he'll kill his new bride as well. He's unrepentant. He'll never stop."

Zeus turned away from him and resumed the trudge up the small hillside. He loaded the weapon into the case in the rear and got into the driver's seat of the jeep. Jeffrey was already in the passenger seat waiting for him.

"It's your responsibility—" Jeffrey began.

"It's not my responsibility! It's the police and the court's responsibility! I won't be a savior to anyone; I'll just be that crazy killer who shot his father!" Zeus screamed. He slammed his palms on the steering wheel in frustration.

"You're concerned about your reputation while children are going to be beaten unconscious and die. Nice," Jeffrey said and turned away from him.

"They know! Why aren't *they* doing anything about it? That's what the law is for," Zeus said. He started up the jeep and pulled out onto the hillside road.

"They've done a great job so far," Jeffrey murmured.

Zeus clenched his jaw and remained silent for the rest of the two hour ride to the apartment. The concrete jaw line he got from his father flexed brutally on the way home.

When they got home, Jeffrey refused to speak to him and just disappeared. Zeus couldn't blame him. He'd hyped up finally wiping that jerk from the face of the earth and then chickened out. He felt absolutely useless.

He retrieved the rifle case from the rear and walked up the two flights of stairs. He walked into his apartment and triple locked the door behind him. He double checked the security system and set the rifle on the couch. He pulled out his buck knife and checked the apartment for any intruders. It was empty as usual. He made a sandwich and sat down on the couch.

He turned on the television and zoned out during the news, more stories of desperation and strife in the world. He snorted as he realized the stepbrother or stepsister that was soon to come would have way more to worry about than getting beaten senseless and tossed into a dumpster. He cracked open a beer and drank it down within moments. He kept the harder liquor locked up with a combo lock, so he was less likely to get after it once he'd had a few too many beers. Tonight was going to be one of those nights. The weekend was going to suck.

Hours later he awoke from his beer fest and stumbled through the dozen or so empty beer cans strewn across the living room. He drank a glass of water and then made his way to the bathroom for an extending pissing session. He looked in the mirror and saw a bruised and bloody face with teeth missing and one eye swollen shut. He shook his head and it reverted back to his normal visage, the only blood was in his bloodshot eyes. He stumbled into the bedroom, dropped onto the bed and fell fast asleep.

"Maybe your father was right all this time," she said as she came into focus. "You always take the easy way out."

Zeus pushed his bleeding head up through the refuse in the dumpster. His whole body ached and he was dizzy. He wasn't sure whether it was the blood loss or the head trauma. He looked down at his hands and they were small. He was twelve again.

His mother sat across from him, discarded food falling from her blood matted hair. He remembered it was always flowing in the breeze. She always kept her hair down, never liking the feeling of it being bound or the tightness of the pull against her scalp. It was one of the reasons his father always pulled her around by the hair while he beat them both.

"I'm not a killer," Zeus muttered.

"Well, that's not true, dear," she replied. The clotted blood that fell from her mouth had already darkened and stained her torn blouse with ugly streaks as it dropped across her chest. "How many did you kill when you were in the service?"

"That's different. They were ordered by the military. Insurgents that were killing innocents." Zeus felt around with his tongue and recognized the shattered remains of the teeth in his upper jaw.

"Is your father so different?" she asked. She raised a grotesquely broken hand to push her matted hair from her face. There was no pain, since she was already dead.

"He's just a chickenshit," came Jeffrey's voice from above. Jeffrey's face grimaced as he looked down from the rim of the dumpster. "This is gross."

"Oh, Jeffrey," his mother said. "Always interesting to see you."

"Yeah, tell me about it. Maybe you can talk some sense into this numbskull. I can't seem to get through to him."

"I don't see how. You're much closer to him than I am," she said as a cockroach crawled from the muck and wandered across her blood stained blouse.

"Not close enough, evidently."

"Tell me, son. Why did you alibi your father for my murder? Did you love him so much?"

"No!" Zeus cried out in his twelve year-old voice. "I hate him!"

"You were scared then?" she prompted. Zeus looked down. He couldn't face her even in the nightmare.

"Yes," Zeus admitted. Tears fell from his eyes. "I'm done with this nightmare. I'm going to wake up now."

"Well, you really tied one on tonight," she said and chuckled. She choked and frowned. She spit out a chunk of flesh. "Oh, seems I bit off part of my tongue while your father was beating me to death. I never realized."

"Let me go," Zeus whispered.

"It's your own subconscious holding you here, dear. Punishment for your cowardice, I think," she said. Zeus raised his head up and noticed her left eye socket had been totally shattered. There were bits of shattered bone and torn eye socket flesh bordering a darkened hole. "I tried to protect you, of course, and it came to this. Dead in a dumpster, blamed on thieves and then you backed up your father's story. I mean, what else were the police to do?"

"He thought killing the insurgents would make this go away," Jeffrey said laughing. "Stupid."

"Did the fights in the bars make you feel like a man, dear?" she said. Zeus hung his head and stared at his own broken arms. How he had survived the horrific beating so many years ago was beyond him. Why he hadn't exposed his father was another mystery.

"I'll just go to jail," Zeus said. "No one will care why I killed him. His wife will just think I'm a cold-blooded murderer and whoever my step sibling turns out to be will just know I took their father away."

"I'm sure it's much better they end up dead in a dumpster like I did, dear. At least their suffering will be over when that happens." She blew the hair out of her face ineffectively and had to use the broken hand to push it away.

"What if I make it look like an accident? Maybe the brake lines go out when he's driving to work or a gas line explosion when he's home alone while she's out shopping?" Zeus asked.

"Sure," Jeffrey chided. "Then what happens if he

survives the accident? He'll know someone is trying to kill him. Who's he going to come looking for? Your chickenshit ass, that's who."

Zeus sat up in bed and promptly vomited all over the covers. He quickly stripped his clothes off and crawled onto the floor into the closet, shutting the door behind him. He shivered there in the darkness until he felt safe again and passed out once more.

Saturday morning brought the filtered sound of morning cartoons on a TV coming from the apartment below. Zeus groaned at the pounding in his skull. He should have grabbed some water after he threw up last night. He'd be regretting it for the rest of the day. He crawled from the closet and the smell of last night's mess assaulted his nose.

"Love what you've done with the place," Jeffrey said causing Zeus to scramble away from where he was sitting on the floor by the door.

"Damn it." Zeus groaned as he held his head. He stood up, bunched the soiled clothing and linens together and tossed them into a basket.

Still naked, he walked by Jeffrey and into the kitchen for a drink. As he gulped the water down, Jeffrey appeared on the other side of the counter.

"You know, I kept quiet so you could get into the military, but I'm not sure I can do that anymore," Jeffrey said. He casually looked at his fingernails as if assessing his need for a manicure.

"Does it matter?" Zeus replied and filled another glass of water.

"They'll lock you away with no chance to redeem yourself. Trapped within your own mind chatting with your dead mother every night. So pleasant."

Zeus growled at him and gulped down more water. He walked out of the kitchen and into the living room to close the drapes. The sun was like a million daggers stabbing his eyeballs.

The door bell rang. Zeus closed his eyes and groaned. He set his glass down and went to answer the door. He unlocked all but the chain and cracked the door open to peer out. His stepmother stood there wringing her hands and looked at him through the crack.

"Zeus?" she said.

"Francesca, what can I do for you?" Zeus said, not opening the door any further.

"Your father," she said as she rested her hands nervously on her very round belly. "He was in a car accident last night. He's at Memorial. They don't think he's going to…" She started crying and shook her head.

"I just thought you should know," she finished and walked away.

Zeus just stood there watching her walk away for

a minute until she disappeared down the staircase. He closed the door and blinked his eyes. His father was going to escape this world without paying for any of his crimes.

He turned around and saw Jeffrey standing there.

"Well, that makes things different," Jeffrey said and winked.

"Does it?" Zeus asked. He walked into the bathroom and climbed into the shower. He turned the cold water on and gritted through the shock as he violently scrubbed his skin and washed his stubbly scalp. He rinsed and got out. Jeffrey handed him the towel.

"Creepy, dude," Zeus said as he took the towel and dried himself off.

"Like I haven't seen you in the buff before," Jeffrey replied and rolled his eyes. He walked out of the bathroom. Zeus looked into the mirror. The bruised and bloody face with teeth missing and one eye swollen shut stared back at him. Zeus sighed.

"It's not over yet," he whispered. He walked into his bedroom, ignored the odor of puke wafting up from the lone basket in the room, got dressed and headed to the front door.

"Don't you need a gun?" Jeffrey said to him as he stood in the way of the door.

"Not this time," Zeus said and walked around

Jeffrey. He unlocked the door and stepped out into the sunshine. His head felt better with the fresh air, although the sunlight was still jarring even through squinted eyes. He trotted down the stairs, got into his car and slapped on a pair of sunglasses to relieve some of the pain slicing through his cranium. Jeffrey sat in the passenger seat, but was strangely silent. Zeus nodded at him and started the car.

The ride to the hospital was peaceful and Zeus even hummed happily as he drove. He enjoyed the wind caressing his scalp and the sun warming his body. He glanced out at the coast far off the road and didn't even mind the sunlight glinting off the surface of the water. Jeffrey said nothing on the way to the hospital.

They parked at the hospital and Zeus went to the front desk. Just to the left of the desk, he noticed a commotion. Francesca was being taken away in a wheelchair.

"Uh, that's my stepmother," he said to the person at the desk. "What's happening?"

"She went into labor when she walked through the front door. Poor dear. The stress of your father's accident, I suppose."

"Where is my father? I need to pay my respects," Zeus said and smiled grimly. He showed his I.D. to the woman at the desk and she gave him the room number.

He walked to the elevator and pressed the 'up' button. When the doors opened, Jeffrey walked into the cab with him. The doors shut leaving them alone.

"This may not do the trick," Jeffrey said.

"On the contrary, I think this is exactly why I couldn't kill him. A single brain shot is an immediate death. No pain, no suffering, and I'd be guilty of murder. This way, he has, in effect, killed himself with his alcoholism. He's just not dead yet."

The door opened and Zeus walked out and down three doors to his father's hospital room. He took a deep breath and opened the door.

A nurse stood by the bed checking the equipment. She turned around and jumped when she saw Zeus standing there.

"Oh!" she said. "You startled me. Are you in the right room?"

"I'm Zeus Promity. I believe that's my father, Eric," Zeus said and smiled thinly.

"Yes, I'm sorry. We're keeping him as comfortable as possible, but… " She frowned.

"It's okay," Zeus nodded. "Francesca told me he didn't have much time."

"The internal injuries were too severe. He'll likely pass within the next few hours. But, he's not in any pain," she said as she pointed to one of the bags hung up near him. "He's on a morphine drip."

"Thank you for caring for him," Zeus said. "Is he awake?"

"Yes," she said as she walked over to Eric's bedside. "He can't respond much as the accident has robbed him of that function, but he can hear you. Mister Promity, your son Zeus is here."

Eric's head moved slightly to one side and Zeus noticed his eyes were taped shut. The tube down his throat was attached to a respirator. Even through the bandages and tape, Zeus recognized his father's concrete jaw line and muscular build.

"He's fairly immobile, but he can respond to your voice," she said. "I'll leave you alone for a moment."

The nurse walked out of the room. Zeus pulled up a chair and sat at his father's bedside. He pulled out the buck knife and traced the morphine drip to just where it connected to the needle in his father's arm. He nicked it ever so slightly and the clear fluid dripped out onto the bruised flesh.

"Hello, father," Zeus said. "I just thought I'd let you know who was responsible for the immense pain you'll experience as you die. The morphine drip will bring you no relief now. You don't deserve to die painlessly. You know why."

Eric's head moved slightly toward him, but he was

otherwise immobile.

"All that muscle you used to beat us, now useless, trapped by an unresponsive body," Zeus whispered. Eric's head moved to one side and then back again. He tried to make a sound but the respirator blocked him completely from any speech. "You deserve every iota of pain you experience before you die and spend eternity in hell. Oh, and don't worry about Francesca—I'll take care of her. I'm sure she'll enjoy a real man making love to her for a change."

Jeffrey appeared on the other side of the bed. He looked down at Eric struggling to respond but only making muted grunts. Zeus looked up at Jeffrey. Jeffrey smiled at him, nodded and then faded from view. Zeus closed his eyes and tears fell freely from his eyes. It was the first time he'd cried since his mother's death.

He only sat there for a few moments before he got up. He needed to go help Francesca through this difficult time. Perhaps they would get together, but it wasn't really a priority. That particular lie was just one last twist of the knife in his father's back.

I don't care if the governor is busy, he can't cancel this!" Eduardo yelled into the phone. He paced around the small living room as he held the cell phone to his ear.

"The virus is just too prevalent," the woman on the other end of the phone replied.

"No, I understand that. I can make adjustments to the masks," Eduardo said as calmly as he could. He looked out the window at the sidewalks empty of movement. The lockdown had been going on for months and even as it was letting up, few people were venturing out.

"The risk is too great and the event has been canceled. I'm afraid our order has been canceled as well," she said calmly. It was clear to Eduardo she didn't care about his well being.

"It's not too much of a risk—it's barely a risk at all!"

"Our lawyers have assured us the risk is too great," she replied.

"I'll sue. You can't do this—it's ninety percent of my business!"

"There's nothing I can do." Her voice betrayed the boredom she felt at the call. It was clear she'd already been through this several times today.

"I have bills to pay. Don't you have bills to pay?" Eduardo walked to the dining room table piled high with correspondence, mostly bills.

"You'll get the standard ten percent cancellation fee just like all the other vendors," she said. "I'm just doing my job."

"Yeah?" Eduardo sneered. "Well, MY job doesn't rob people of their livelihood!"

"Goodbye, Mister Estanza," she replied and there was a click.

"Hello? Hello?" Eduardo pulled the phone away from his ear and looked at it. The call had ended.

"Son of a bitch!" Eduardo shouted at the phone. He raised his arm up to throw it across the room when his eyes caught his wedding photo on the mantelpiece. His mood softened and he shoved the phone into his pocket. He walked over to the photo and lifted the frame off the shelf.

Darla looked so happy next to him on the beach

under the wooden arch with the flower spray just behind her. Her bright blue eyes stared at him from a world away, telling him it would be alright. His mouth almost curved into a small grin, but even the promise of her love couldn't change time. He set the photo back on the cold hard surface and returned to the table behind him. He moved through the paperwork in a kind of fog until he found the bill from the cemetery. Seventy-five hundred dollars was still due before they'd put her in the ground. The Halloween extravaganza was his big income earner for the year. Fifty thousand dollars would've set him up for the next year even with Darla's funeral expenses. Ten percent wouldn't even cover the balance due on her funeral. She'd be above ground for months, never at rest unless he could accomplish a miracle.

The vultures at the funeral home had already drained his savings with down payments and body preparation costs inflated because of the pandemic. Now things were finally lifting, businesses were opening back up. The business loans and everything else he'd done to get through the absence of business over the last year was going to come due and, instead of a big chunk of business the government promised, he'd have a pittance to deal with it all.

He walked numbly into the garage he'd converted into a workshop. He glanced around at the boxes of supplies he'd gotten for the extravaganza. They were all still sealed. He'd be able to return everything but then what? The house, his workshop, and probably even his truck would all be gone. Everything repossessed to pay the creditors off.

He looked at the desk. It was covered with sketches and notes for his new designs. He'd added N95 level protection, HEPA filters and even respirators for some of the masks. Everyone at the extravaganza would be safer than if they were home or at a grocery store picking up milk. It was all for nothing.

His eyes were drawn to the garage door. There stood his prototype with a state of the art respirator system, enclosed in a fearsome hooded figure. Faux blades lined the arms as this modern day grim reaper would deal death from the forearms instead of a scythe. He walked over to the costume and lifted the skeletal mask from the hook on the mannequin. As he turned it over in his hands, he blinked at the open connections where the respirator hoses would fit, hidden underneath the black and tattered robe.

He set the mask down on the table behind him, next to the power tools he used for the mass production of costumes and support systems. A set of brushed steel legs lay on the table, parts of a structural support system for a hanging box that someone would've sat in at the extravaganza. He cocked his head as he looked at the metal and then turned his head to look back at the grim reaper's arms. The faux plastic blades were just the right thickness to be replaced easily by some machined metal blades.

He walked over to his desk and grabbed a pencil and some paper. He grabbed a stool and sat down next to the steel legs. He used his measuring tape to find the length and width. If he cut it along the one side, it would leave a lip to attach to the leather arm braces. He ran some figures on the strength required for the leather and determined he'd have to beef it up a little to support the brass grommets he could bolt the blades through. He took a marker and drew the cut marks on the flat steel. He returned to the plans he'd drawn and added some notes about supply needs including some drill attachments for sanding the blade to a sharp edge. When he'd finished he looked at the plans and shuddered. He could slaughter a normal person in seconds where they stood. The blades could cut a jugular as easily as they could cut a tendon or ligament. Simple flesh would fall before the blade. No one was prepared for this in everyday life.

"Darla, what's happening to me?" Eduardo whispered. He sat frozen on the stool staring at the work before him. He closed his eyes and the last six months flooded into his mind. The deaths from the virus decimated his immediate family. He'd fought with his parents to be safe and they kept screaming at him that he was a sheep falling for the pandemic hoax. They all thought it was overblown. None of them took precautions until it was too late. First his grandparents passed. His parents rationalized it as inevitable since they were old. They were likely to die anyway. When his uncles and aunts came down sick, his father said they should've taken better care of themselves. Overweight or suffering from other ailments, one by one his entire family succumbed. They all died alone in a hospital room.

Most frightening of all was when his father, the last to die, was loaded into the ambulance. He looked Eduardo straight in the eyes and said "It was God's will."

When Darla had fallen ill, the most likely cause was that she was trying to save his father's life. She was a nurse at the hospital. Even with her own frustration at his family's refusal to wear masks, she still fought to the very end to save his life. Even when she realized his last visit with both of them had been without a mask. Stubborn to the end and it had cost Eduardo everything he held dear.

Two months of deterioration in a hospital room alone. He got to talk to her, not with her, a handful of times while she languished on a hospital bed in a coma, moist air pumped into her lungs by a machine.

"Did she even know I talked to her? Did she even hear me?" Eduardo murmured to the workspace before him.

"I heard you," a soft voice replied, causing Eduardo to look up, startled.

She stood just across from him, her pale skin nearly the same color as the hospital gown she wore. The deep, dark circles under her bloodshot eyes stared at him. Even as he felt his heart melt at the sight of her beautiful eyes, he also felt the guilt overwhelm him.

"Darla," he whispered. He shook his head, but she remained, her very existence an accusation of abandonment he couldn't avoid. His mind swam back over the years to Hawaii where they said their vows. A picture perfect moment years before politics and tribalism had brought this country to ruin.

"They still live," Darla said plainly.

"What?" Eduardo asked, not sure he'd heard her correctly. His mind still hung onto the happy memories of their engagement, marriage and honeymoon.

"You will avenge my death, won't you my love?" she asked sweetly. Eduardo looked down at the drawings he'd done. The modifications would be deadly indeed. His arms would cut down anyone who stood before him. Eventually, someone would stop him. A gun would ring out from a corner as the inevitable police response took him down. But that was if he didn't plan his strike well. Do it on Halloween when there were dozens of costumed people on the streets. He'd be forever hidden among the throngs of people who would ignore social distancing. They would run by in their costumes, frolicking with their fellow teenagers. Hundreds of children and their parents filing along the streets, visiting neighbors and spreading their contagion with wild abandon.

Yes, in that crowd, he'd be hidden in plain sight. They'd even cheer him as he walked from his last kill, actual blood dripping down his blades. Perhaps there would be other tissue or even brain matter clinging to the metal or staining his robe. And they'd all think it was part of the costume.

He sat up with a gasp as he realized he'd nodded off right there in the chair. The drawings remained. He shook his head in fear. He looked up, but Darla was gone. Had she ever been there? He didn't know anymore.

"This is madness. Nothing will bring her back."

He jumped up from the chair and ran from the workshop. He clattered through the door and stumbled down the hallway to the bathroom. He turned on the water in the sink and splashed it on his face until his shirt was soaked.

He looked into the mirror. Was he a killer now? Is

this how it happened? Someone at the end of their rope with nothing left to lose drowning in a pit of darkness ends it all by becoming a murderer? He felt like he was a shell of himself. His head dropped as the pounding threatened to break open his skull. His insides ached with the pain of loss. The emptiness from his despair felt like a dozen daggers slowly turning within his stomach.

"They're all fine in their private towers, laughing at our loss while they have the best of care," he sneered at the sink. He looked up at the mirror again, dark tendrils of wet hair plastered across his face. His eyes, once vibrant and full of life, now stared back at him with nothing but black emptiness, all pupils and no iris.

"They're insulated. Forever out of reach of the real danger," Darla said. "They'll never feel our loss... unless you make them feel it."

Eduardo turned and saw his love standing in the bathtub, half hidden by the shower curtain.

"I'll be hated. I'll be a killer," Eduardo said to his dead spouse. Her head cocked to the right and she smiled.

"Who is left to care, my love? They've taken everyone." Darla smiled sweetly, her thin blue lips revealing black stained teeth. "Even our unborn child."

Eduardo looked back at the mirror and set his hands on the counter. His right hand came to rest on the skeleton mask. Had he brought it with him from the garage? He didn't remember grabbing it.

"You're not real," Eduardo whispered. "This isn't real."

"I'm within you, my love," she replied. "I'll never be away from your heart. They can take my life, they can crush my body to putty, burn my flesh to ash, but they can never take me away from your memories."

"I can't become a killer," Eduardo said. He looked at Darla again. Her flesh had turned green with decay. Her hair sloughed off from her scalp. Black bile dripped from her mouth. He gasped.

"You see what they've done to me, my love," Darla said, her voice harsher and garbled from the liquid drowning her tongue. "You must avenge me. Teach the killers that they will be punished for their transgressions. It's your duty as my husband. They can't get away with it."

Eduardo's eyes fell to the floor. Bits of his wife fell to the light green carpet, staining it with dark liquids he could only assume were coagulated, rotten blood. He fixated on the putrefied bits of flesh laying there, imagining his love's body falling into the same state of decay inside the funeral home.

"They'll just let her rot," he said and wiped the sweat from his upper lip. "Like all the others. It's just a money grab. Bleed the families dry. They've already taken all the money from the rest of my family to bury them, why not the last bits of cash I have to my name?"

He clenched his fists and realized one of them held a hard object. He looked down and saw the skeleton mask in his hand. He didn't remember picking it up.

He blinked his eyes and looked back at the shower. His wife's decaying body struggled to stand as the last bits of flesh fell and the bare skeleton shivered and swayed. A single bony hand rose up and he heard her voice one last time.

"Punish them as they have punished us, Eduardo!" Her voice issued forth from a bony maw. Then, the steaming skeleton collapsed onto the piles of dark meat writhing with maggots and flies.

Eduardo stared at the carnage in bathtub for so long, he couldn't remember if it was day or night. All sense of time fell away, as he lost all sense of self. Eventually he raised his eyes to the frosted bathroom window and realized day had given way to night. He turned his head to look in the mirror again. His face was pale and drawn. He'd had no food or drink all day, but he felt neither hunger nor thirst. He slowly turned until his body faced the mirror. He raised the mask slowly to his face and pressed it to his flesh. It fit like a glove. It gave him the warmth and security he could no longer find in life. It thrilled him like the warm embrace of a lover; the only true affection he could feel now that his world had been destroyed.

He secured it to his head and cocked his head to look at the reflection.

"They want to cancel Halloween?" he whispered and grabbed the edge of the counter. "I'll give them a Halloween to die for."

# PROGENY

**S**hane held onto the cold porcelain for dear life as his body dry heaved for the umpteenth time that morning. He'd never been so sick from drinking before.

He was due at the airport in six hours for the first leg of his journey home from South America. Just the thought of getting on the small charter plane to Rio de Janeiro made his head spin which led to the inevitable retching that followed. He tried valiantly to think of absolutely nothing.

Two hours later, he crawled from the bathroom and struggled to open a bottle of water. The lukewarm liquid felt like heaven drenching his cracked lips and parched throat. He downed the first bottle quickly and popped open a second. Hydration, he decided, would be the best cure for this truly monumental hangover. He wondered briefly if it was the amount of alcohol he'd consumed or if he'd managed to pick up something from the water he'd been diligently avoiding consuming. He decided it was probably alcohol since Miguel had introduced him to the local tequila blend last night and he had no recollection of how much he had consumed.

He sat there, leaning back on the wall by his bed for a while. As his body regained its balance, he felt the weariness weighing him down. Food seemed a poor choice at the moment, so he finished the second water bottle and opened a third. In addition to the general ache he felt all over, a dull throbbing pain just beneath his right shoulder blade reminded him of the strange incident at the club last night.

As he'd toasted his fellow private security colleagues around the table they stood at, a drunk or something had bumped into him. The bump had been accompanied by a sharp pin prick just below the shoulder blade. He remembered turning to see the stranger who had bumped into him. His first impression had been that the man wasn't all there. A vacant stare met his before two of his coworkers had pushed the assailant away.

His training alerted him to the possibility of being poisoned, but this job in country had been passive at best. There was simply nothing to engender an assassination attempt in this locale or any job he'd been on for several years. Besides, Miguel had assured him the drunk was a known local and an inebriated stumbler of great renown.

Shane pulled himself off the floor and climbed into bed now that the room had stopped spinning. He set the alarm on his cell phone and was asleep as soon as his head hit the pillow.

Hours later, Shane felt like warmed over shit as he climbed into the prop plane with seven other passengers. He packed light to begin with, so his baggage was minimal. He turned off his cell phone to conserve battery, bunched his light coat into a ball and put it under his head to try to rest on the way to Rio. However, rest was not to come so easily.

The small plane and requisite turbulence was its own level of hell. While he only used two barf bags on the short two hour flight, the same couldn't be said for the entire plane that was affected by his near constant retching and the unpleasant odor that minimal air circulation did nothing to dissipate. Between the sound and smell of his purging, two of his co-travelers were sympathetically ill. He gained no new friends on that flight.

He scored some Dramamine in the larger international airport in Rio. He had an hour for it to take effect before they began boarding for the flight to Miami. Mercifully, the medication broke down fairly quickly, filtered into his bloodstream and Shane finally got some rest. He slept so hard the flight attendant had to wake him up for disembarking.

Shane was sore but felt immeasurably better having gotten nearly eight hours sleep on the flight. As he stepped out into the sunshine, heat and humidity of Miami's late summer, he smiled. He hadn't told Danielle exactly when he was getting back, but his return trip wasn't exactly a secret. She could have looked the information up on her own. Just the same, after eight months away, he hoped he didn't surprise her while she was with another boy toy.

When he reached her apartment thirty minutes later, he was greeted by an enthusiastic girlfriend assaulting him with a hug and deep kiss that made the trip worthwhile in an instant. He was glad he brushed his teeth at the airport because she was doing it again with her tongue. Her taste immediately brought back the fun they'd had over the last five years to his mind. After some intense making out in the foyer, she finally let him pick up his bag and close the door.

"I'm glad I didn't interrupt your time with another man," Shane said as he stepped into the living room.

"Well," Danielle replied as she strutted around the apartment, showing him every angle of her barely clad body. She hadn't let up on the workouts and Shane felt he might need to step up his game. He'd gotten a small paunch from his time out of country. He probably put on five pounds and she looked like she'd become even more trim and fit than he remembered. "He left hours ago. I mean, someone had to take your place in wherever doing whatever it is you do."

"Lucky him," Shane said as he pulled her close. He was well muscled and, though he'd gained the weight, it was just as likely she didn't notice or care. He ran his fingers through her long dark hair and marveled at her tan complexion. She hadn't missed a tanning day or a workout. "I left him half a bottle of shampoo and a shower cap."

"So thoughtful," Danielle said as she stripped off his clothes and then her own. "We don't need no stinkin' shower cap."

The next forty-five minutes were a blur of flesh, desire and intense anaerobic activity. Eventually, their lovemaking took them to the bedroom. Much to his surprise, Shane passed out on the bed when Danielle went to freshen up in the bathroom.

She let him rest and resumed her work in the living room on her laptop. She knew exactly where he'd been. They'd met through work. She was a recruiter and, though she didn't work for the company he did anymore, she knew what line of work he was in. She also knew it could take a lot out of a person, even someone who took incredibly good care of their physique like Shane. A few hours later, she'd finished booking enough business to pay her own bills for the next year. That would give her a well needed break to spend with her beau.

She walked back in and roused him from his slumber. He groaned into the pillow as he lay on his stomach.

"Did you get in a tussle before you got on your flight?" she asked as she stroked his lower back.

"Not really," Shane replied. "Why?"

"You have a bruise on your back next to your shoulder blade. It's purple, but yellowing like it's a few days old."

Shane turned over and sat up.

"I had a little run in with a drunk on my last night at the going away party. Nothing real intense. I don't even feel it."

"OK. I'm sure it's nothing," Danielle said. She kissed him and they returned to their intimacy. "It certainly hasn't slowed you down."

Shane stopped her before they got too far.

"I better check in with Jeremy before it gets dark. He'll have a fit if I don't," Shane said as he lifted her off of him and she stood before him and pouted.

"Jeremy," she said as she undid her robe and her naked body peeked out. "What's he got that I haven't got?"

"My paycheck." Shane smirked and ran back into the living room. He dug his phone out of his coat and turned it on.

While he waited for it to power up, Danielle walked into the kitchen and pulled out some food. They could both use a snack to power them through the night.

When his phone finally came up, he frowned.

"Huh," he said to Danielle as she brought him a plate of chicken and edamame. "I have a few voicemails from Brazil."

He put the phone up to his ear and listened to the voicemails. Danielle puttered around as he frowned and shook his head.

"I can't make heads or tails of this. I'm going to have to call him back."

"What is it?"

Shane looked at her and shrugged.

"He said something about a Mikalla zombie, doctor and a man on fire," Shane said. "It doesn't make any sense."

"Something lost in translation?" Danielle asked as she sat down and opened up her laptop.

"I don't know. Let's find out." Shane pressed a few buttons on his phone. He put the phone on speaker.

"Hello, Shane?" the voice on the speaker said.

"Yeah, it's Shane. I'm back in Miami okay. I got your messages, but couldn't understand them exactly."

"You need to get to the doctor right now," Miguel said.

"I feel fine. Whatever illness that guy had, I clearly didn't get it."

"No, Shane, you don't understand. They have to cut it out of you before it's too late. They had to burn Diego to stop the infection from spreading. You have to go now before it's too late!"

"Whoa, slow down Miguel. We don't just walk into a doctor's office in America and tell them to start cutting. I need to know more."

"Diego was a Mikalla zombie. They had to burn him before he could spread the infection to the entire town."

"Burn him? Like kill him?" Shane frowned.

"They burned him alive in the town square with flamethrowers," Miguel said.

"Jesus!" Shane exclaimed. "That's a little extreme."

"Get to the doctor now!" Miguel said.

"Calm down. I'll make an appointment and go see my doctor."

"You don't have time for an appointment, compadre. Make them see you now," Miguel said.

"Shane," Danielle said. "You need to look at this."

"OK, Miguel, I'm calling the doctor right now. Talk to you soon." Shane hung up the call and looked at Danielle. She looked frightened.

Shane walked over and she turned the laptop screen to him. There on the screen, they were holding a woman down as they cut open her finger from the tip down to the bottom knuckle. A bulbous white worm poked its black tipped head out and swayed around. The doctor grabbed it with a set of tweezers and three smaller dark brown tendrils darted out from around the worm and attacked the tweezers with stingers. The flesh inside the woman's finger had been hollowed out by the worm to make room for it and the three things attacking the tweezers.

Shane's jaw dropped open as the men holding the woman down took a nail gun and secured her hand to wooden board. There was very little blood. From around the nail holes, Shane noticed the head of another little attack worm poking out of the punctured flesh.

In a swift motion, one of the men quickly hacked the woman's arm off mid forearm. Jets of blood squirted out all over the place and the woman fell backwards. A man standing by stepped up and took a flamethrower to the woman's severed hand and the board, burning everything to ash.

The video then cut to a few days later with the woman sitting in a hospital bed and a bandaged stump where her hand had been. She smiled grimly at the camera and then the video stopped.

"Holy shit," Shane said. "That's just available on the internet?"

"Classified file on Mikalla eradication," Danielle said. "It's a BSL-4 contagion, Shane. We have to get you to the doctor now. Miguel wasn't shitting you."

"Fuck me," Shane said. "Let's go."

Danielle grabbed her keys and they ran to the elevator. As the elevator opened, Shane's phone rang again.

"Hey, Jeremy?" Shane said as they stepped onto the elevator. "I'm back in Miami, yeah. Got a little medical issue. Some kind of Mikalla infection I've never heard of before. I'll let you know what's up when we're done. Better mark me off the schedule for a few weeks until we get this sorted out."

The elevators doors closed and Shane suddenly dropped his phone.

"What the hell?" he said and then grabbed his right arm in pain. Little brown worm heads erupted from his right and middle index finger. Shane screamed in pain. Danielle reached for him, but Shane jerked away from her. He slammed his hand onto the emergency stop button.

"Get off the elevator!" Shane screamed at her. "Before it's too late!"

Danielle pried the elevator doors open and crawled out into the opening leading to the sixth floor. She fell onto the ground.

"Shane!" she hollered and the doors closed before he could respond.

"Shit!" Danielle hollered as she ran for the stairs.

Shane fought against his right hand moving of its own accord, the worms looking for anything they could attack, but strangely not Shane himself. Finally, the worms retreated back into his hand. He marveled that there was no blood.

Then, the pain erupted in his skull. He raised his right hand to his temple as he fell to his knees. He screamed as it felt as if his head was coming apart. Then everything went dark and Shane fell to the floor.

When Danielle arrived at the elevator on the first floor just a minute or two later, she pressed the call button. The doors opened and the elevator was empty. She looked around, but couldn't find him. Shane was gone.

She took out her own phone and tried to make a call, but there was no signal. Just then, armed men dressed in black emerged from the parking garage and came in through the other entrances to the building. Danielle sighed as she slid her phone into her back pocket. A man with a single white stripe on his left lapel walked up to her.

"Where is he?" the man said.

"Jeremy," Danielle said. "Best black ops could do on short notice?"

"Where is he?"

"I don't know," she said as she looked down. "Something happened to him on the elevator. He shoved me out and when I reached it from the sixth floor, he was already gone."

"He's a biohazard," Jeremy said.

"I know," Danielle said as she fought the lump in her throat.

"Search the building and don't forget the elevator shaft!" Jeremy shouted to the others and they immediately fanned out. He pulled on the small microphone on his lapel. "Have B team go over the schematics on the sewers and tell me when we have eyes in the air."

"Brazil?"

"Contained. They were doing the contact tracing when Miguel clued in the containment team. We found out an hour ago. Sorry we didn't get here sooner."

"Shane... he and I..."

"Yeah." Jeremy nodded. "We'll get you checked out. You're probably fine, but if we don't find Shane in the next twelve hours it will be a moot point."

"Why is that?"

"The original infection point was a village of eight hundred people in Mikalla, Nigeria. A man went the full course of infection to the spore stage and... well, they burned the entire town and everyone in it from the sky. Blanketed the area for ten square miles with napalm."

"We have to warn everyone. Evacuate them," Daniele said.

"To where? We're not going to be able to evacuate nearly three million people in under twelve hours anyway. We have to find Shane before he completes the transformation or Miami gets nuked in twelve hours, whether we find him or not."

At first, Shane could only make out shadows. After a while, his vision began to clear and he could witness what his body was doing.

He watched in horror as his hands reached out from behind a man and twisted his head, snapping his neck. He realized he was moving through a warehouse, killing people as he went. He'd thought the creature controlling him would sting people like he had been in Brazil, but there was a calculation to the movements. It took him a moment to realize what was going on. The creature was accessing his memory and his abilities to reach a goal. It had an agenda beyond simple infection of a few random people.

He concentrated and tried to take control back of his body, but there's was no purchase for his intellect to latch onto. There was nothing he could do but observe. His body functioned like an automaton under the control of someone else. Two more people died before he figured out he was in a factory of some kind. A water treatment plant, perhaps? He couldn't access any of his senses besides sight and he only caught fleeting glimpses of machinery, but it was enough for him to ferret out the details.

He struggled to understand why a water treatment plant. Could this entity infect people through the water supply? Had it just never had access to a centralized water supply before? South America was in many ways a third world country. Water treatment wasn't common except in the larger cities. Even then, it wasn't the best or completely trusted. But it was trusted in North America.

His body suddenly jerked to the right and Shane could see red lights going off. Someone had tripped an alarm. Without another thought, he was exiting the building and disappeared into the deep brush behind the plant. He was making his way northward toward the center of Miami-Dade County.

He struggled to recall if he'd witnessed what the entity had made him do at the plant that might infect people. Try as he might, he couldn't recall much before he started to see the limited things he could. He wasn't sure if the entity was allowing him to see it or it had just lost control of this part of his psyche. He hoped against hope that he was fighting the infection off and maybe his body was winning the fight to repel the invader.

He wasn't sure how much time had passed, but he could see the sun was getting low in the sky. He wondered if the entity would need sleep. Would he have a chance to regain control when it did? Would he commit suicide to save others from infection if he had the chance? He thought he would.

The entity walked calmly into a large apartment building. He noticed himself looking around the building, checking for cameras. This building was unsecured. Anyone could walk in undetected. The perfect place to hide as his subconscious would be informing the entity.

He entered the stairwell and began climbing the stairs. As he ascended, the pace slowed. Shane theorized the entity may be tiring. He may have a chance to get control soon. He waited for his opportunity, probing anything he could with his mind.

The passage of time became difficult to track in the windowless stairwell. But when they emerged on the roof, it was night. The wind was at his back, blowing towards the big city, the most populated area of Miami. He could see the big hotels and apartment buildings in the distance. He looked to his right and saw lights and helicopters surrounding the water treatment plant. He realized the entity had accessed his mind to do exactly what he would have done—create a distraction.

His arms went up in the air and they spread wide. Shane began to get some feeling back in his body as his chest split open and a billion spores erupted from his chest cavity into the night air.

A lone helicopter caught him in its spotlight. It hovered there for a moment and then the light went off.

The night was dark again until a blinding light engulfed Miami and the surrounding miles under a nuclear mushroom that Shane only got to see a glimpse of before he joined everyone within ten miles becoming so much ash.

# HAVE A DRINK

ave you ever killed someone?" the ginger haired stranger asked.

Daniel frowned at his beer. He glanced at his questioner just a few feet away.

"What a strange thing to ask," Daniel said as he raised the mug to his mouth. He took a deep drink of the cool golden liquid. The piped in satellite music changed from a raucous punk song to a classic rock tune.

"So that's a 'no' then?" The stranger sipped an amber liquid from his much smaller glass. Daniel guessed it might be a bourbon whiskey and that he might need something stronger himself if this nutcase kept at it.

"Neither confirmation nor denial," Daniel replied as he smirked. It was still quite early in the day. The regular crowd wouldn't fill the dusky dive for hours. Daniel and the stranger were the only ones sitting at the bar. The dark corners of the tiny business held maybe one or two more patrons.

"It just seemed likely you had given your general disdain for life," the stranger said and raised his hand to the bartender. "Another please. Make it a double."

Daniel fixed his gaze on the strange man. He evaluated the black leather coat and decided it was upscale. A button down red shirt with no tie, but likely a designer brand; it seemed flawless and comfortable. The color was a bold choice, but given the stranger's hair, it seemed to complement his looks well. Daniel noted the hands were manicured, so he likely took care of himself and probably wasn't a physical labor type. With a physically trim build, it was more than likely he saw the inside of a gym multiple times a week. Perhaps, Daniel mused, he was simply a well-off, muscle bound dope. Trust fund moron, most likely. Daniel relaxed. This day drinker would give him about as much trouble as a house fly.

"I'm not a cop, if that's what you were thinking," the fit man said.

"It wasn't and I couldn't care less," Daniel replied.

"Still," the stranger continued as the blonde bartender delivered his second drink. "We're all governed by certain inevitable laws, aren't we?"

"Whatever," Daniel said and ordered

another beer.

The two sat in silence for a few moments before one of the other patrons in the bar walked out. Daniel happened to glance the man's way. The third man paused at the door, turned to glance at Daniel and gave him a respectful nod of the head. Daniel gasped. The man had pure red, glowing eyes and a grey pallor to his skin like a gargoyle. The grey man smirked at Daniel's reaction and then walked out the door.

Daniel shook his head and rubbed his eyes.

"You've got the perfect job," the stranger said as he dragged the complimentary bowl of peanuts next to his drink. The dull scraping sound seemed amplified in the nearly empty room. The piped in music had gone silent.

Daniel glanced around the room as he wondered where the bartender had disappeared to. It seemed like the room was absent of all life except for himself and the chatty barfly. Daniel squinted into the darkest booth in the place, but couldn't tell if it held a person or just shadow.

"Everyone does what suits them," Daniel murmured and took a drink of his beer.

"Ain't that the truth? But, I wasn't talking about how you made money. I am a great admirer of your other handiwork."

Daniel glared at him.

"Maybe you've got me confused with someone else."

The stranger nodded and chuckled. It was a deep, ominous chuckle with just a hint of threat to it. He pushed back from the bar with a grating metallic scratch of barstool on concrete. He popped a few peanuts in his mouth, stood up and raised his glass to Daniel.

"Record sales in real estate, Mister Madrid. I'm well aware of your day job, as you portray it," the stranger said as he took a sip of his drink and walked around the bar top. He stopped next to Daniel. "It's your art that I'm most enthused about."

"I sell big houses to rich people. I don't have a hobby," Daniel said and turned back to his beer. He considered its heft as a weapon; the thick glass might last through several bludgeonings on a troublesome stranger's skull before it broke.

"Hobby? No, Mister Madrid. I refer to your true calling in the arts of homicide."

"I'm afraid I don't follow," Daniel replied dully. He took a drink as he calculated the proper trajectory to hammer home his displeasure at the direction the conversation had taken.

The stranger stepped behind Daniel and moved back into the room between the small tables, outside the range of a simple swing of a beer mug.

"The old man on the subway, strangled and then the eyes meticulously removed. Your first instance of leaving the body in a public place, if I recall correctly."

Daniel took another drink. He inventoried the bottles within reach behind the counter. A bar fight would be a great cover to end this simpleton's prattling.

"Now you really sound like a cop," Daniel replied smugly. If the stranger really was an investigator, Daniel mused he was trying to bait the wrong fish. Daniel let his eyes nonchalantly survey the room for hidden cameras. Just as likely it was audio only. He wondered which judge had authorized it. Even more concerning—had he gotten sloppy? What evidence had been left behind to warrant this kind of intrusion. His mind raced over each crime scene.

"What intrigues me beyond your delightful penchant for bloodshed, of course, is why you close your own eyes when you pop your victim's into your mouth. Never chewing. Always swallowing them whole."

Daniel's mouth hung open as he was dumbfounded for more than a few seconds. He quickly composed himself and looked down at the ice receptacle.

"Your joke is in poor taste," Daniel said. He took a quick drink and returned to his inventory of the available weapons at his immediate disposal. A corkscrew hung on the rear wall, just out of reach. There, though, near the beer taps by the bowl of lime slices was a medium-sized knife. He figured he could dispatch the stranger fairly quickly with the blade. If it was sharp enough, he could take his trophy as well. Probably have to off the barkeep as well and torch the place to cover his tracks. Was there surveillance? If it was a sting, though…

"Poor taste? Funny observation coming from a human who consumes his fellow human's flesh."

"You clearly have me mistaken for one of your other suspects, detective…?" Daniel replied. He took a deep cleansing breath. If this guy was a cop, he'd have backup. He couldn't just take him out. He had to play it cool. A clean exit was best, no matter how much he wanted to cave this guy's head in.

"Detective, no. Demon would be much, much closer," the stranger said. The music overhead suddenly sprang to life with Johnny Cash singing about death.

Daniel bolted for the door, but it was stuck fast. He gave it a few hits with his shoulder.

"Your work with the Mulligan twins was inspired. I mean, forcing the girl to watch you kill and dismember her brother knowing all the while she was next. The horror on her face was… delightful. Her fear… well, I'm just sorry that you as a mere mortal couldn't taste it. It was as divine as you would find a filet mignon prepared rare—a creamy, bloody consistency that melts in your mouth.”

"I want a lawyer, cop. I ain't saying anything. This is entrapment, kidnapping, illegal detention. You have to let me go." Daniel strode to the bar and grabbed the knife. He turned to face the stranger who hadn't moved from where he watched Daniel.

"Again, I'm not the police, so you can't have a lawyer. Although, we certainly have enough of them in our retinue, it wouldn't be hard to get one here," the stranger said as he set his drink down and pulled a cigar from his jacket. "Whiskey goes so much better with a Cuban, don't you think?"

The stranger held the cigar in his mouth with his left hand as he held out his right and produced a small jet of flame from his right index finger. He lit the cigar with the fire and took a few puffs before the dancing light at the end of his finger simply went out.

"If you're not a cop, why are you here? To send me to hell?" Daniel scoffed.

"Not yet, my good man! Patience. You have such a bright future of carnage and delicious terror ahead of you. I'm a real fan. You are some of my best work, after all." The stranger sat down in a chair and kicked his feet up on another.

"Best work?"

"You remember your first kill? You'd thought about it for months just off the slightest suggestion I put in your mind the night your father killed your mother."

Daniel's face went from a healthy shade of indifference to a pale reflection of shock. That murder so long ago had sent his father to prison for life. The only real benefit was the beatings he suffered at his hands stopped to be replaced by the less effective punishments of his less capable uncle. It was a common oversight by child protective services, delivering a child from one abusive household to another and closing the book.

But the thought, that small gem of murderous intent had surfaced that night as he listened to the violent interactions happen below in the kitchen while he hid in the attic. The thought that she was weak and deserved what was coming. Then his thoughts had traveled to one of his classmates; she deserved the same, but he'd never said a word.

"No one else knows that," Daniel whispered.

"I watched her murder, of course. Clumsy execution. Your father had brutality on his side, but no real style. You know, panache."

"Did you make him kill her?" Daniel asked as he gripped the knife in his hand tighter.

"Make him? No. We find talent, nurture it, and

nudge it along. A stray thought here, a flash of inspiration there, anything to move the process along."

"We?"

"What's the opposite of a heavenly host, a devilish host?" The stranger chuckled. "Anyway, there's a dedicated team. If we do our job right and get lucky enough to find prolific talent with a penchant for torture, we really do reap the benefits. When your soul drinks in the abject fear of an innocent, oh my, there really is no better ambrosia in all of eternity."

Daniel sat down on the barstool. The knife hung limply from his hand. He blinked at the stranger and wrinkled his nose.

"So, why are you here now?" Daniel asked. "Fan club meeting? You want my autograph?"

"A bit of preventive maintenance, I'm afraid. You, my prolific, deranged genius are dangerously close to getting caught." The stranger dropped his feet from the chair and sat up. "I'm here to remind you to not get lazy. You need to step up your game."

"Let's say, hypothetically, that I'm this homicidal maniac you think I am," Daniel replied. "You want me to be more careful?"

"No. I want you to be more clever," the stranger said as he leaned back and took a big puff on the cigar. "You remember Alan Strahan? The way you forced his head onto the train tracks, neatly obliterating his skull? You made it nigh impossible to link his death to your other harvests. You need to alter your signature even more. Dismemberment, dissolving the body in acid or spreading the parts around the forest—mix it up is all I'm saying.

"Change how they're killed?" Daniel asked.

"No, that's not necessary. Although, if you want to mix that up, have at it. It does play hell with the forensic investigators. Frustrating them is its own special enjoyment. But, no, when it comes to your method of executing your hobby, I personally enjoy the hell out of the fear and torture. It's such a feast of the most delicious, darkest emotions every time. You really are an artist. That's all you, by the way. Credit where credit is due. I remember suggesting your first kill, but your enthusiastic performance was, for lack of a better word, breathtaking. You're a natural. A true homicidal aficionado."

Daniel retrieved his beer from the bar and took a big swig. He remembered the first kill like it was yesterday. Catherine Montaglio, his first crush and ultimate rejection. The thrill wasn't in the hunt or capture, but in the way she perished at his hands. The way her eyes rolled back in her head over and over again each time he brought her to the point of death and back again. It was the only time he completed the kill before cutting out the eyes.

Ten years later, she remained in that shallow grave in the desert, undiscovered, but always there for him to revisit should he choose to. That had been his first real accomplishment in meticulous planning. He'd spent months scouring the land records for land that was completely worthless in every way. It had to be too far from anything to accidentally become a land development of any importance. No mineral, soil or other valuable asset to be gained from touching the land. Just empty, barren desert. He realized that was what the stranger was talking about. He'd become complacent. If he didn't change his ways, he'd become sloppy. He didn't relish the idea of spending time locked up for being an incompetent idiot.

"So, you're just sitting around reaping the benefits of a few seconds work when I was twelve years old?" Daniel asked as he turned around to look for the barkeep.

"You always were one of the most brilliant I've ever nurtured. It's not all fun and games, unfortunately. I do what I can to deter the guardian angels. 'Don't kill that girl. She's innocent. That young man has a bright future ahead of him. Spare his life.' There's also the early 'don't skin that insert-animal-here.' They are so pesky sometimes. Drowning them out for the early initiates is a trying task. It gets easier as the subjugates get older and stop listening to that little voice."

Daniel thought back to the moments just before he ended Catherine's life. A faint whisper had tried to dissuade him from going through with it, but his desire to see her finished was too great, his hunger too powerful. That drive, that inner beast was only too much fun to engage and entertain.

"So, my quixotic, demonic observer, any other advice?" Daniel asked as he set down his empty beer.

"Kill as many as you can," the stranger said seemingly directly into Daniel's ear. The hairs on Daniel's skin pricked up all over his body as the stranger's tone had changed from jovial to dark and menacing. Daniel whirled around and the stranger had disappeared. An empty glass sat on the table where he'd been sitting, a still burning cigar resting on the rim.

"What the hell?" Daniel whispered.

The front door of the bar burst open as the first patrons of the evening crowd began to arrive. The bartender walked over to the empty whiskey glass and picked it. She turned to Daniel and smiled ever so briefly, her eyes flashing red just for a moment.

"Your tab is paid in full, Mister Madrid," she said.

"We look forward to your continued patronage."

Then she walked behind the bar and resumed her normal activity.

# PAYING THE PRICE

That's not how magic works," Selena said as she folded her arms.

David sat back in his seat and cocked his head at her curiously. He'd always liked her bleached pixie cut, but he had to admit the longer, curly neon blue was growing on him. It contrasted her hazel eyes well.

"It's what they deserve," he said. He picked up his soda and unscrewed the cap. "A public service, really."

"Evil begets evil," Selena replied. She started to pack up her tarot cards. "No matter your intention."

"It's justice," David said as he shrugged his shoulders. The gesture moved his long dark locks in a way that made Selena weak in the knees.

"Please don't mess with darkness. You'll release something you can't control," Selena said as she put the cards in her bag. She leaned forward and put her hand on his knee. "I care about you. I don't want to see you get hurt."

David patted her hand gently and winked at her.

"I care about you too. Stop worrying. Everything will be all right."

Selena sighed. Her heart felt like it would burst through her chest whenever she was around David. But, it was clear he didn't feel the same. His passions centered on revenge not romance.

"Let the positive outweigh the negative," she said as she stood. "If you only do good things—"

"You'll get crushed under the malevolent feet of your enemies," David said quickly, his lips flattened to a thin pink line.

Selena gasped and closed her eyes. After a moment, she opened them and looked into his pale blue irises.

"Promise me you won't do anything," she said. "I have to go to work. We can talk about it again tonight."

"I am a paragon of virtue," David replied, grinning.

"And a smart ass," Selena smirked. "Just promise me you'll leave the darkness alone."

"I'll do the best I can."

Selena shook her head. She put her hand on his cheek and forced a smile.

"I'll see you soon."

She walked out the door and, as she climbed into

her car, she looked back at the house with concern.

David was already at the door. He waved and smiled. Selena smiled and closed the car door. David watched her back out of the driveway and pull out onto the street. His smile dropped into a scowl.

"I've already danced with darkness and came out virtually unscathed," he whispered. He rubbed his left shoulder absently where the skin had turned a dark red. The epidermis had become dry and scaly, but nothing a little lotion couldn't fix.

He drained the last of the soda and turned toward the kitchen. A shadow passed across the doorway, nearly imperceptible.

"You'll serve me again soon," David said. "I know you hunger."

David walked to the refrigerator and gathered some items. He grabbed a few more from the pantry. Had Selena done a thorough inspection, she may have noticed a few items of concern. He had concealed most of it very well and she'd never looked. She thought he was still contemplating action, still thought of him as an initiate. He'd hidden his ambition almost as well as he'd hidden his darkest impulses from her.

He carried his supplies to a closet door and opened it carefully. He shoved the hanging clothes out of the way and slid the fake wall to the side, revealing an open doorway.

"Light," David said to the darkened doorway and several light bulbs spring to life via a voice activated system. He maneuvered carefully onto the steps leading down and made his way to the basement.

He set his small burden down on a table near the base of the stairs. On the wall behind the table, five pictures hung, tacked into place haphazardly.

Two women and three men—the cabal of cronyism, David called them. Architects behind his despair, they all conspired to pull the levers of power to drive his humble curio shop out of business. For months, he toiled away at his altar, pulling every positive spell from his grimoire that he could think of, even going so far as to attend city council meetings to plead his case. All for naught. The increased rent, the new business restrictions and eventually changed zoning laws all designed to drive him from the shop he'd work for ten years to get off the ground. Positivity had gotten him evicted from his shop and all his product confiscated.

For all her positivity, Selena was right about one thing—evil does indeed beget evil. They'll never know what hit them.

He pulled the bloodstained picture of the second woman off the wall. She was a middle-aged woman, chubby cheeks with a winning, business professional smile. He had pulled her picture from a charity website she was on the board for. They all wore their chameleon skin so well.

"Your power couldn't stop that cement truck, Angeline. Your hoity-toity body crushed beyond all recognition. You'll rest six feet under in a steel drum, so much sanctimonious soup," David said, hissing the last part. He picked up a lighter from the table and lit the picture on fire, watching it burn for a few moments before dropping it into the small metal trash can against the wall. Flames licked up the inside of the receptacle briefly before fading out, finally becoming nothing more than a plume of smoke.

He pulled the next picture off the wall. It was a middle aged man with a well trimmed beard showing more of his gray than his hair. David wondered if the affliction to the man's black hair was due to a guilty conscience. The list of businesses ruined by this local developer was more numerous than the hairs on his head, gray or otherwise.

"Your wealth can't protect you from the darkness you embrace, Franklin. The homeless you put on the streets, the owners put out of business drinking themselves into a dark pit, and the countless suicides are all on your hands. Luxury cars, private yachts and vacation homes abroad. Where, I wonder, does your avarice end? At the very least, I'll know when."

David took the picture with him to the large pentagram painted on the floor of the basement. He set it down near the top and retrieved the other items, setting them all nearby. Next, he retrieved a freshly sharpened kitchen knife with a six inch blade. It glinted in the light coming in through the basement window. David grunted.

He pulled the room darkening curtains across the tiny window. His elusive friend in the shadows was clearly mischievous. He thought about securing the drapes in a more permanent fashion, but then his friend would just undo that as well. He glanced again at the pictures on the wall.

"Only a few days more," he said. He lit the candles arrayed around the pentagram. They were already partially melted and affixed to the bare cement floor.

He reached into the fish tank against the far wall and retrieved a long snake.

"Time to repay me for all the mice I've given you," he whispered to the small python.

"Light," he announced and the bulbs in the basement went dark.

He unbuttoned his shirt just enough to let the snake slither inside to enjoy his body's warmth for a few moments. With a sigh, he settled into the center of the painted symbol and began the incantation. As he spoke, shadows emerged from the darkness, forms just a bit deeper in inkiness than the surroundings. They circled around him until he finished the spell. He pulled the snake from his shirt and picked up the knife. He held the snake over the picture.

"You wish to open the doorway again?" a voice hissed from the darkness.

"Yes," David responded, holding the snake firmly.

"You are... willing to pay the price?" the undulating shadow inquired.

David swallowed hard. The hand holding the snake began to shake.

"I am," David whispered.

"Proceed," the voice said in a whisper that echoed throughout the blackness.

David swiftly cut off the snake's head and the still writhing body spurted out blood on the man's picture, the floor, and down David's arm.

Where the blood touched David's skin, it seeped into his body and burned. David dropped the still twitching snake and grabbed his arm. He cried out in pain and felt the skin on his upper back harden and blister. Blood, his own this time, trailed down his back, soaking his shirt and waistband.

David screamed and passed out.

A few hours passed before David awoke, face down on the basement floor in a pool of his own blood on top of a dead snake and the crumpled picture of Franklin Dunworth.

David stuck the picture back on the wall with considerable effort, his movements stiff and halting. Pain screamed from the torn, burning flesh on his back, every action a searing dagger of blinding, white hot fire in his spine.

When he ascended the stairs and entered his kitchen again, it was still daylight. Even filtered as it was, the light burned his eyes. In combination with his blistered flesh, the pain was overwhelming. He stumbled to the sink and lost the contents of his stomach. In between heaves, he screamed in pain. It only lasted minutes, but felt like an eternity. Luckily, the mess was easily cleaned by simply running the water and garbage disposal.

After securing his basement sanctum, he shed his clothes and climbed in the shower. He barely glanced in the mirror, catching just a glimpse of the ruined flesh on his upper back. The dried rivulets of blood would wash away. The wounds the blood came from wouldn't disappear so easily.

As the warm water cascaded across his broken

skin, he ground his teeth. How could he make it through the other three sessions? Would he even survive the next one? He cried as the searing pain ravaged his broken mind. And yet, he persevered.

He turned off the water and laid the towel gently across his shoulders, patting the flesh dry tenderly as one would a sunburn. He hoped the stinging would subside, but felt it was unlikely. Like the pain from his previous "payment," it seemed the agony would fade only very slightly but remain a constant reminder of his journey for justice.

Steeling his nerves with a deep breath, he looked in the mirror and surveyed what he could of the damage wrought upon his flesh. It was more than damage. It was growth.

His shoulder blades sported new nubs of flesh poking out about two inches. He flexed his back and grimaced at the pain. The new growth appeared to be both bone and tissue. It was hard to tell amidst the blistered, scaly skin, but he deduced it was more than just swelling.

David stared at it for a good long while. This was more than a painful skin irritation. He didn't quite know what to make of it. For a few moments, he was too stunned to notice the pain. That didn't last for long.

He searched around for some antibiotic cream

and applied it the best he could. He rummaged around in his dresser for a T-shirt he wouldn't miss and slid it on. It stuck to his treated wounds immediately. He threw on another T-shirt and added a flannel shirt open at the front. He checked himself in the mirror and decided a disheveled appearance worked better than having to explain the trauma to his back.

He made a quick meal and noticed the light fading. Selena was running a little late. Perhaps he should be relieved. It would mean fewer questions to navigate. He could just rest and hopefully heal.

Half an hour later, his hopes were dashed as he saw headlights pop up on his garage door. He sipped his tea as he waited for her to walk in and ask how he was doing. It was the normal banter. He sort of looked forward to it like a favorite comfy blanket.

When she came storming in and slammed her bag down on the table, he jumped back in his chair and had to suppress the wincing.

"What have you done?" she demanded. She stood with her hands on her hips staring daggers at him. He looked down at his cup of tea.

"I brewed chamomile. Should I have gone with peppermint?"

"Franklin Dunworth is dead," she said plainly. She watched his eyes and he smiled.

"Well, I'm certainly not going to shed a tear if that's what you're waiting for," David sipped his tea and sat back casually. He regretted it immediately as his shoulders touched the chair and he winced again.

"What's the matter with you? Why are you in pain?" Selena asked.

"I just pulled a muscle in my back," David said. "Do you want some tea or did you just come to yell at me about a coincidental, fortunate death of a scum bag?"

"His yacht blew up while he was pulling away from the dock. Everyone on board perished." Selena clenched her jaw.

"Do you think I put a bomb on his yacht?" David scoffed. "I wouldn't even begin to fathom where to ask for such a thing. Besides, I've been here all day. I'm certainly not keeping up with that dickweed's sailing schedule."

"You think you're clever, David?" Selena asked. "Angeline Hartford is dead too. Freak car accident with a cement mixer."

David pursed his lips. He never should have mentioned his ire for his mortal enemies or their names.

"A morbidly fascinating coincidence," David said as he got up to refill his tea. "Nothing more. Are you sure you don't want some chamomile?"

She came up behind him and innocently touched

his back. It was meant as a gesture of caring, but the pain was like a lightning strike. David dropped his tea cup and it shattered on the floor. He ducked away from her and shuffled across the room.

"What's wrong?" she asked, her anger replaced by concern.

"Nothing," David said as he stayed just out of reach.

"Your back?"

"Leave it! Just leave it alone," David growled.

"David," Selena said. "I can feel the darkness growing. It's stronger now than it was earlier. You have to stop—"

"I don't have to do anything," David responded with a menace that caused Selena to take a step back. "Everything is predestined. We don't make the choices. They're made for us."

"We choose our own destiny, David," Selena said.

"Not when an army of evil is arrayed against you, Selena. To fight injustice and stop it in its tracks... you have to take some shortcuts."

"David, you can't take the easy way out—"

"Do you think this is easy?" David spit the words out like they were poison. "Get out!"

Selena grabbed her bag. She rushed to the door, but turned to him with grim determination.

"I can't let you finish this."

"Really?" David laughed. "Do you think you can wave a few daisies around and make it all better? Go back to your tarot cards and tea leaves, Selena. Leave the heavy lifting to people who can handle it."

With tears in her eyes, Selena turned and stormed out the door.

He watched her go with a tinge of regret. He took a deep breath as he fully realized the finality of their parting. He had to complete everything tonight. She may not be able to stop him, but he had no doubt she knew people who could.

They could affect his memory, strike him dumb or cripple him in some other way so he could no longer do the incantations. There could be no delay.

He wished he had a chance to rest, but then he probably wouldn't be able to sleep anyway. Getting it all done now was for the best. If rest could come, it would after he was done.

He gathered whatever else he needed for all three rituals and went over in his mind how to combine all three. He had the animal sacrifices at the ready, the words came to him easily and the darkness was more than willing to assist. He wondered briefly on the true cost to his health and well-being. The prize was worth the cost even if that cost was his life.

Urgency energized him like he hadn't been for weeks. He'd been laconic since they'd torn his business away from him. He'd wallowed in self-pity for way too long. This renewed sense of purpose would carry him through. Everything was crystal clear suddenly.

Down in the basement, he pulled the remaining pictures, placing them together but splayed out at the tip of the pentagram. He placed the two rabbits in a small box he could easily reach and tucked the last snake in his shirt as he had before. As he wove the words of the three incantations together, the shadows assembled as before but with an increased intensity.

"Mortal," the dark voice boomed, shaking the building. "Do you wish to open this doorway forever?"

"Forever?" David asked.

"The aid you seek will lock this portal open. Do you wish to commit to this act?" the voice boomed, no longer the subtle hissing that had gone before.

David stared at the shadows as they undulated and pulsated before him. He'd come this far, he couldn't turn back now. Justice had to be served!

"Do you wish it?" the entity hissed.

"Yes!" David hissed back.

"And..." The darkness paused. David held his breath as he waited for the next inevitable question. "Are you willing to pay the exorbitant price?"

David closed his eyes as he realized his life and soul may be forfeit after tonight.

"I am," David whispered.

"Excellent," the shadow said and laughed low and dark. "Proceed."

David pulled out the snake, cut off its head, and blood spurted out on the pictures below. He grabbed the rabbits and simply slit their throats, the joined blood spilling all over the pictures and himself. He waited for the pain to overcome him, but nothing happened.

"The price..." David whispered. "Why haven't you taken me?"

The darkness chuckled.

"You're bound by ritual to Selena, the incorruptible. Did you really think we wanted you? We already have you."

"Selena? No!" David shouted.

The shadow laughed and David felt everything go dark as he collapsed on the cold, hard floor.

#  LOOP

reg walked into the old time saloon and took a quick look around the room. The tables were populated by patrons dressed in cowboy garb of varying styles drinking out of old style glasses or mugs depending on their personal poison of choice. As he navigated the crowded establishment, all eyes were on him and none of them seemed friendly.

Greg sat down at the south end of the bar and noted his own clothing should help him fit in with this seedy, hick crowd. He sported the same era dusty boots and brown pants. His vest seemed a bit newer, but it still carried the stains of not quite bleached cowhide. He didn't sport a hat but noted the other guy a few seats down did along with a long leather duster and another set of cowboy boots. There didn't seem to be any other kind of foot covering in the place. Other than the indifferent gaze of the bartender, the guy at the other end of the bar was the only one not giving him a gaze of hatred. The unshaven man nodded at Greg with a tip of his broad rimmed ten gallon hat and then took a drink from his small glass of dark brown liquid. Maybe not a friendly face, per se, but at least not a hostile one.

Greg cocked his head as he watch the stranger swirl his glass around and a darker black cloud seemed to reach out from within and caress the inside of his glass for a moment before disappearing back into the rich brown depths.

"Mornin,'" the man said to Greg as he winced through swallowing the drink. Greg guessed the swill this guy was guzzling must be pretty strong. He briefly wondered why someone would drink it at all if it caused so much discomfort. Then his mind traveled back to some of the alcoholics he'd known and he stopped wondering.

"Beer," Greg said to the barkeep who had also dressed the part in this odd western Greg had walked into. He sported a striped canvas shirt, black pants and the ever present cowboy boots.

"You sure?" the bartender asked, raising his jet black eyebrows. Greg figured he probably waxed them. That was something they did in the old west, right?

"Yeah," Greg replied and frowned. The bartender shrugged and filled a mug from a plain looking keg sitting on a shelf behind the bar. He handed it to Greg. Inside the golden liquid floated the same swirling ink-like substance that he'd seen in the dark liquor the other man drank.

"What the—" Greg started.

"It's sin," the man at the other end of the bar said. "Well, the physical manifestation of your sins with regard to him." The man then pointed to a sepia tone picture framed on the wall at the back of the bar.

"Who is that?" Greg asked. "I don't know him."

"He's the reason you're here. Same reason I'm here."

"I'm just visiting," Greg replied as he swirled the beer and watched the strange liquid inside the beer move with a seeming life of its own.

"Wishful thinking," the man replied and the entire bar broke out in raucous laughter.

The man looked out at the room and sighed. He turned back to Greg.

"Better drink up or face the alternative," he said and took another drink of the dark liquid, wincing once again. He sniffed and blinked his eyes. "I recommend the firewater next time. It isn't sour, burns better and masks the sin just a hint better."

"I'm not drinking that! Did it come from the bottom of the barrel?" Greg said and set the warm mug down on the rough, varnished surface of the bar. The man shook his head and stared straight ahead.

"They always gotta learn the hard way," he said and sighed. The other men in the saloon laughed darkly as the bartender just shrugged again and continued polishing the mug in his hand with a bar rag.

A man in black pushed open the swinging doors of the saloon. He raised a revolver in his hand and pointed it at Greg.

"One bullet," the man in black said. Greg turned and looked at the man as the other men in the bar echoed his ominous words.

"One bullet," they all murmured in unison. Then the man fired the gun and Greg's chest erupted in crimson as the bullet tore through his flesh. His left ventricle was shattered and his stricken heart leaked blood like a broken water balloon. Greg fell to the ground as his precious life supporting fluids briefly pumped out of him. As his heart stopped, the precious bodily fluid lost all pressure and drained slowly out of his major organs. He gasped for breath and then stopped trying as the energy seemed to drain out of him faster than his blood. His body went into shock and his head rested on the hard, dusty floor. His eyes stared straight ahead at the rustic ceiling until everything went dark.

Greg walked into the old time saloon and looked

around. He blinked and grabbed his chest. His flesh was restored. There was no bullet hole, no blood and no torn flesh. He looked at the lone man sitting at the bar. He looked behind him, but couldn't see the man in black anywhere. He turned back around and the bartender looked up briefly and then went back to polishing mugs.

"This is insane," Greg muttered. He turned around and walked out of the saloon.

Greg walked into the old time saloon.

"Shit," he shouted.

The men at the tables all chuckled and went back to their drinking.

Greg pursed his lips together and backed out of the saloon.

Greg walked into the old time saloon. He threw his hands up in the air.

"What the hell?" he exclaimed.

"Now you're getting it," the man at the bar said as he raised his glass in a toast, drained the entire glass and then buckled over in extreme pain. No one moved to help him. They sat at their tables drinking normally with no discomfort at all and ignored the man's distress. The bartender calmly poured another glass of the dark liquid and set it in front of the struggling man.

"This is insane," Greg whispered. He slowly walked up to the bar and took his seat again.

"This is some kind of trick. There's two identical rooms or something. Where's the real exit?" Greg examined the walls behind the bar looking for hidden cameras.

"Really?" The other man picked up his new drink. "How many times have you been shot dead and resurrected moments later?"

"Beer again?" the bartender asked while twisting his lips into a smirk.

"Yeah, I want beer again and cold this time!" Greg hollered.

"You see any ice?" the bartender said as he poured another warm beer from the tap.

"Isn't there a mini fridge under the bar? Why does this place have to be so damn authentic?"

"It's a metaphor," the other man said. "Old time frontier justice for your soul."

"That's very poetic and a load of bullshit," Greg said. He took the beer as it arrived. The same swirling dark substance hung in the beer like a storm cloud. "What does this stuff do anyway?"

The other man took a deep breath and took a small drink from his potion of sin. He shuddered as he swallowed.

"It burns the soul," he said as he coughed a bit.

"Well, how fucking stupid would I be to drink it

then?"

"If you prefer dying over and over again, knock yourself out. I prefer measured pain over unpredictable trauma."

Greg pushed the beer toward the bartender.

"Serve me a beer without the black shit floating in it."

Without a word, the bartender took another mug, pantomimed filling it and set the empty vessel in front of Greg.

The front doors swiveled open and the man in black entered. He raised his gun and pointed it at Greg.

"One bullet."

"Are you fucking kidding me?" Greg replied. He swung his arm forward with the mug and threw it at the man in black. The gun fired. The bullet shattered the mug, ricocheted off a spittoon on the floor and struck Greg in the back, puncturing his right lung.

Greg collapsed against the bar. The men at the tables laughed as he slid to the floor, a crimson trail darkening the front of the bar behind him. The pain was excruciating. Every breath hurt. Greg clutched at the open wound as the air gurgled in his chest with each blood soaked breath.

"Call nine one one," Greg gasped. Again, the men at the table laughed. One of them stood up.

"Nine one one bullet!" he hollered and the room shook with laughter, dust falling from the rafters.

"You see a phone, genius?" the man at the bar replied. "The bullet never misses. Have fun bleeding out."

By Greg's pained estimation, it took nearly fifteen minutes of pain and agony before he began to feel light headed from loss of blood. The pain continued for another twenty minutes or so before his heart seized up and blood stopped pumping completely. Moments later, everything went mercifully dark.

Greg walked into the old time saloon and looked around before he could stop himself.

"Son of a bitch," Greg said as the men at the tables all scowled at him and then began laughing.

Greg grit his teeth as he took his spot at the bar.

"Beer," he said simply. The bartender dutifully poured him a warm one with the customary sin injection. Greg poured it out on the bar and ran to the side of the front door, empty mug in hand. He stood there for several minutes, controlling his breathing and calming himself. Then he heard it.

"One bullet."

The voice came from behind the bar. Greg swiveled his head to look at the bar and saw the man in black standing behind the bar. He raised his gun and Greg ducked.

The bullet tore off a piece of Greg's skull and he stumbled around the saloon holding in his brain with his right hand while blood streamed down his arm. He bumped into the men at the tables and they just pushed him around the room like a pinball until he finally passed out.

Greg walked into the old time saloon and sighed.

One of the men at the tables started singing 'pinball wizard' and the room erupted in laughter again.

Greg walked slowly to the bar. He raised his hand to the bartender and nodded. The bartender poured him another and brought it to him. Greg sipped the beer and scrunched his face up in disgust. Just a moment later, he doubled over in pain as every cell in his body felt like it was on fire. The blinding pain took his breath away and he found himself gasping for breath about a minute later when the pain subsided.

"Okay, that sucked and the beer is sour."

"Welcome to the authentic old West. I told you the firewater was better," the other man said as he took a drink, grit his teeth and clenched his fists.

"How often do you have to drink?"

"To keep the grim reaper away? Roughly every five minutes or so."

He stared straight ahead for a minute or two,

seeming to zone out for a while.

"Sometimes, I just set the drink down and let it happen to break the monotony."

"Where does he usually shoot you?" Greg wrinkled his nose as he took another drink. As he grasped the bar in pure agony, his mind likened the feeling of his cells bursting to being struck with lightning… again and again.

"I don't get shot. It's the noose for me." He pointed at a worn timber overhead. "They usually toss it over that. I was a hanging judge in life—only fitting that's my punishment here at the hands of a posse."

"Judge?" Greg asked.

The judge pointed at Eldon's picture on the wall.

"I was paid well by Eldon to cover his crimes. Had a crooked D.A. that delivered framed people to my court. Some of them were put to death."

"Well, I don't know him," Greg said. "I don't know why I'm here."

"Oh, I know why. I'm the judge that kept you out of court at his request." The judge took another drink and squeezed his eyes shut. After a few moments, he opened them again.

"We had a nickname for you—Minority Report."

Greg took a deep drink of the venomous concoction. This wasn't a discussion he wanted to have.

He relished the pain blocking out everything else, the blood rushing through his ears and the stars obscuring his vision. When he surfaced again from his lagoon of pain, he heard one of the men behind him shout "Minority Report" and they all laughed long and hard.

"You really gave us a challenge keeping you away from the long arm of the law. Ironic since you were the law. Racist with a badge. Shoot minorities first, ask questions never. You caught Eldon red-handed in mid flagrante, shall we say, raping some poor Hispanic woman at knife point. And you didn't shoot him. You let him walk with a nod and a smile. Then you shot his victim so she couldn't identify, testify, or anything. He told me everything. That's why your subsequent crimes were covered up. You deserve this just as much as I do."

Greg said nothing but just sat there staring at his beer. The black cloud within the golden liquid seemed to pulsate, laughing at him. He didn't deserve this.

"They all deserved to die," he whispered.

"Yeah, I used to think that too," the judge said. "Until I experienced closing time here at the old saloon."

The judge stared ahead again, his humorous, cavalier attitude a distant memory. He looked down at the cloud within his own drink and seemed hypnotized by it.

"What happens at closing time?" Greg asked.

"These boys at the table behind us rise up and shed their human skin, revealing their true nature in various demonic forms. First, they'll nail us to the wall. When we've been well secured, they'll pierce our flesh with their talons and shred it for each sin we've committed. Then they'll tear the flesh from our bones, harvest our organs for sport and then break every bone in our bodies. We won't die just yet. We'll exist in a world of searing pain and misery until we finally expire at sunrise."

He looked over at Greg and for the first time, Greg could see the haunted look deep within the judge as the light faded from his eyes.

"Then the day starts all over again."

Greg turned to look at the men surrounding them in the saloon. They all looked at him with glowing red eyes, raised their drinks high above their head and laughed maniacally.

**S**ure, Doctor Tobias was it? It's Saturday, I've got a few minutes," Cheryl said as she opened the door for the middle aged man with graying hair. She thought he was a little young to go gray; maybe he didn't handle stress well. Her critical eye noted his suit wasn't designer but just 'nice.' Nails poorly manicured, possible he bit them and he was unshaven as well. Perhaps he presented better during the work week, but he wouldn't last a day at her company.

Doctor Tobias stepped into the foyer and raised his bushy, untrimmed eyebrows.

"Nice place," he said simply as he walked to the left into the elegantly furnished living room.

"Thanks," Cheryl said curtly as she shut the door. At least he didn't smell. She self-consciously tugged her tight fitting shirt down and tucked it back in to the waistband of her black yoga pants. Somehow, she'd put on an extra pound or two in the last couple of weeks despite regular workouts. It irritated her that this unplanned imposition had further delayed the intense workout she was about to start to remedy her minimal weight gain. She wanted to look pristine for the board meeting Wednesday; the anticipated sale of her company would come with an obligatory photo op.

Doctor Tobias glanced around the room and nodded as he waited. Cheryl walked in and waved at the sofa.

"Sit, but don't expect to stay long," Cheryl said as she sat down in a leather recliner.

"Of course," he said as he took a seat on the couch closest to her. "I'll get right to the point. I know you're a busy and very successful woman."

Cheryl rolled her eyes. If this scraggly brainiac was going to come on to her, it would be a short meeting indeed.

"You recall your, ahem, visit with a Mister Erich Tanner?" Doctor Tobias said delicately.

Cheryl sighed. She'd told no one, so Erich must have been very proud of his conquest. She could imagine the burly man sitting around a sticky tavern table raising his beer to his buddies as he regaled them with her submission to his lustful advances.

Even as she thought back to that night, her pulse

raced. His eyes, as dark as night, drew her in. She couldn't understand her attraction to the tall, muscular brute, but she couldn't deny it either. He'd simply come up to her as she stood there with her girlfriends on her rare night out.

"Hi, I'm Erich," he said. She turned to him and somehow melted immediately. Her jaw hung open and for the first time in her life, she was speechless. The bar and everyone in it seemed to disappear. It was just her and Erich, alone in a heated fog of sexual urgency.

Erich gently pushed her jaw closed and bent down to kiss her. The world exploded in her mind. Everything, every thought, evaporated leaving just her and her new love. He took her hand and walked her out of the bar before her friends realized anything.

They got in a cab and furiously made out in the backseat. She didn't remember if she or Erich had given the cabbie her address, but it didn't matter. As soon as they crossed the threshold of her front door, she was on him like an animal possessed.

He picked her up like she was nothing and carried her to the bedroom. Once there, his calm demeanor changed and he matched her feral nature. Clothes were torn, skin was scratched and flesh was bitten. The sexual tornado they created in that room destroyed furniture, tore curtains and shattered windows. They consummated their lust a dozen times before she collapsed.

Erich left her a puddle of exhausted flesh, spent in every way possible, passed out on the bed. If he'd spoken another word since the bar introduction, she didn't remember it. All she remembered was the all-consuming lust that had taken over her. She chalked it up to a lifetime of repressed sexual urges, even though she'd never been the least bit interested in anyone before. Pursued by a few, but none had even touched her lips before that night.

The next morning, she found a single hand written note on the kitchen counter.

"I'll see you again," was all it said.

"I recall," she said to Doctor Tobias. "Has he been bragging?"

"I haven't the slightest idea," the reserved man replied quietly. "I'm just familiar with his pattern."

"Pattern? What kind of doctor are you anyway?"

"Anthropologist. I've been following Erich for several months."

"Well, Doctor Tobias, if you're here to talk about his sexual conquests, that just makes you a pervert."

Doctor Tobias chuckled.

"I'm much more interested in stopping him," Doctor Tobias said and folded his hands in his lap. He looked at her expectantly.

"From having one night stands, aren't you the chivalrous hero?" Cheryl said as she relaxed in the chair. Snark was a specialty she'd developed over years of business squabbles and tough negotiations. She'd had her share of head to head confrontations with men asserting their alpha dominance. It was always a pleasure to see their surprise when a woman wasn't immediately cowed by their brusk manner.

"You are a self-made, self-sufficient woman, yes?"

"The sale of my company has already been announced, Doctor. My net worth isn't exactly a secret."

He nodded.

"Confident, resilient and self-sufficient are Erich's most sought personality traits in the women he seeks," Doctor Tobias said.

"How clinical of you," Cheryl said. "You know, some people consider me attractive as well."

"No doubt, you're beautiful," Doctor Tobias said. "It is one of his considerations, but not his sole requirement for selecting a brood mother."

"Brood mother? What the hell are you talking about?" Cheryl sat up. She gripped the arms of the chair, ready to bring out the dominant executive.

"Erich is a different breed of human, if you can call him that." The look of disgust on the doctor's face told her more than perhaps he intended. Jilted lover?

"Jesus, a guy who has a one night stand is not another breed of human, doctor, although I'm sure their egos would argue otherwise," Cheryl said as she stood up. "I'll see you to the door."

"You're pregnant," Doctor Tobias blurted out and looked down for a moment. He took a breath and then looked back up at her. His jaws were clenched.

Cheryl stood stock still and narrowed her eyes at him.

"How did you know that?"

"You've never had a one night stand before, were likely chaste before your encounter with Erich and you're pro-life, unlikely to have an abortion," Doctor Tobias stated.

Cheryl walked toward him fists clenched.

"How do you know any of that?"

"Erich's criteria for his mates. Also, a clean bill of health and will fight ferociously to protect their children."

Cheryl folded her arms.

"I haven't told anyone I'm pregnant. I have a doctor's appointment to confirm the test on Tuesday."

"I need your help to stop him," he told her again.

"Why my help?"

"He will likely kill me outright, but a brood mother

would have a certain level of protection from his wrath," Doctor Tobias said. "He'd be just as protective of the unborn child as you are, possibly even at the expense of his own life."

"Why do you need to do anything?" Cheryl asked. "Surely one man can't do that much... damage."

Doctor Tobias lowered his eyes and stared at the floor.

"I've interviewed twenty-seven women in this region, all impregnated with Mr. Tanner's progeny," he said.

"That's a lot of child support," Cheryl said, chuckling. "They can sue for money I suppose, but what's illegal about it?"

"He's not entirely... human."

"Huh. He seemed plenty human to me."

"How many one night stands have you had other than Mr. Tanner?"

"None," Cheryl replied, shifting from one foot to the other uncomfortably.

"How many sexual partners besides Mr. Tanner?"

"That isn't your concern," Cheryl said.

"I'll wager the answer is none, just like the other twenty-seven women. Saving themselves for marriage. Don't you think it's curious they all met him for one night and slept with him?"

"So," Cheryl laughed, "your fiancé cheated on you with Erich? But she wouldn't give it up for you?"

"That isn't your concern," Doctor Tobias replied icily.

"The hell it isn't!" Cheryl yelled. "You show up at my door and try to convince me to kill a man just because he banged your girl? Seems it's exactly my concern! Why doesn't she help you?"

"Because she's dead," he whispered. The energy seemed to drain out of him. Cheryl felt sorry for him, but it didn't quell her rage.

"Did you kill her?" she asked.

"No," he replied quietly. "Suicide. She couldn't live with what she'd done. What he'd done to her. It wasn't even her fault."

"It takes two to tango, doctor. I wasn't forced."

"Did you really feel like yourself? In complete control?"

"I felt... alive. There was no thought, just emotion and desire," Cheryl said. She walked back to her chair and sat down. "He initiated the first kiss, but after that, I was the aggressor until... it was very surreal."

"He mesmerized you, hypnotized you somehow."

"It didn't feel like that. It felt like, for the first time in my life, I was truly alive. Every emotion burned like fire and filled my soul like nothing before. Hardly anything like hypnotizing." Cheryl closed her eyes and thought back to that night. She remembered everything in perfect detail—the emotions, sights, smells and the feeling of Erich pressed against her in primal, carnal ecstasy.

She opened her eyes and saw the pain on his face. He looked wounded like she'd hit him with a brick. She could guess why.

"And she knew she'd never feel that with you or, any other man... but she loved you," Cheryl said. "And every other woman who had a partner in her life would feel the same."

"If he creates enough like him, they'll simply take over the world in one or perhaps two generations. Mankind forever changed. If we can kill him, monitor the children, maybe we can stop the spread." Doctor Tobias returned to his clinical self.

"Monitor the children? Never mind, I don't want to know. Look, I don't even know how to contact him." Cheryl shrugged. "Why would he come back to me?"

"You're both linked and he'll try to protect you," Doctor Tobias said.

"But I'm not in any dan..." Cheryl trailed off as she saw the gun emerge from the doctor's coat.

"You're in mortal danger," he said as he stood and waved the weapon toward the back door. "Into your car, please. We're taking a trip to a little cabin I have."

"Shit," Cheryl murmured. She got up and mentally kicked herself. She'd never met this man and let her guard down. Now she was going to be a statistic. She wondered if he was a serial killer.

"Is your name even Tobias?" she asked as they walked to the back door.

"Of course it is," he replied. "I didn't lie to you. I'm sorry it's come to this."

They got into Cheryl's Mercedes sitting in the driveway. As the car started up, she turned to him.

"You know the police can track this car; they'll know where it's been," she said as she pointed back to the house. "You're on camera, Doctor."

"I don't care," he replied. "I'm not trying to get away with anything but killing Erich Tanner. You can be a witness at my trial, if you like. But they'll have to prove he's human and I'm pretty sure they'll be unable to do that."

She pulled the car out of the driveway and ground her teeth together, resigned to this fate at least for the moment.

"Which way, *Doc?*" She added the last sarcastically.

"Up the mountain. About a ninety minute drive."

Cheryl took what she thought would be her last

look at her little Tudor mansion. She took a deep breath and drove down the street.

As she turned onto the highway, she thought maybe a little reason could sort out the good doctor's broken heart and derail this revenge plot.

"Certainly couldn't hurt to discuss this with Erich in person. Work out this little misunderstanding."

"Really?" Doctor Tobias smiled thinly. "You think saving the human race should be negotiated over a coffee and pie?"

"Maybe you have dinner first?" Cheryl grinned and then lost the smile when she saw the frown on his face.

"My paranoia is not as farfetched as it might seem, Miss Benning. They did a DNA test on the fetus at the autopsy," he said.

"So you could identify the father?" she asked.

"At first, they weren't even going to do an autopsy, but I told them the father should be notified."

"Clever," Cheryl said. "Is that how you tracked Erich down?"

"No. I already knew his name, but I didn't tell them. They were confident at first that they could get a match. But then, when they got the results back, they said there was no viable DNA from the fetus and they couldn't tell me anything more." Doctor Tobias looked out the passenger window as the scenery changed from suburb to farmland dotted with trees. "I hacked the lab and got the results. The DNA was part human, part something else. I recognized some strands as similar to canine DNA, but everything else was completely alien. The pictures of the fetus… it looked like a normally developing human. Nothing to suggest the DNA was out of the ordinary."

"You should go to the authorities," Cheryl started.

"Before I had completely looked at everything, there was a gas explosion at the lab. Three-story building gone. Everyone dead at the scene. Not that they could find much left of them."

They rode on in silence for a while. Doctor Tobias was again distraught and kept gulping, choking down his emotions.

"I'd gone to school with several of them. Two of them were close. Would've been at our wedding."

"I'm so sorry," Cheryl said. "What did the police say about the explosion?"

"Federal government locked down the building and the investigation. Claimed classified work was taking place there. Not a word since. Complete blackout."

"Was that the Pika Institute?" Cheryl asked. The details were sketchy at best about what happened. An explosion followed by brief news coverage and then nothing. His delusions were grounded just enough by facts to make them plausible. The hairs on her forearms rose as the air in the vehicle seemed to chill.

"I never believed in conspiracy theories until I lived one," he said quietly. "Take the next exit, then left."

Cheryl glanced in the rearview mirror. There were barely any cars on the road, certainly nothing close behind them.

"I don't think we're being followed."

"He can find you, perhaps by scent or some other connection to you. He won't let any harm befall you."

"I'll take your word for it right up until the bullet enters my skull," Cheryl said harshly.

"It won't come to that. The question is, will you step up when the matter is at hand?"

"The matter, as you put it, is still up for debate," Cheryl said.

"When he bursts through the door, will that convince you?"

"You're the one with the gun. That really makes you the dangerous one in this scenario," Cheryl replied as the engine whined. The road inclined at a steep grade.

"Not for long, I assure you," he said as he pointed the gun to the road in front of the car. "Turn right up here."

"I take it I'll get a quick death at your hands,

then," Cheryl responded. "At least that's somewhat reassuring."

"Mercy is a fading pleasantry."

Cheryl turned onto the gravel road and grimaced. If she lived, the Mercedes would probably need a new paint job. It was going to be an expensive Saturday.

Half a mile up the road, a small cabin emerged from the woods. The area was well-kept, brush and grass trimmed back with scattered branches piled up for easy access. Cheryl mused that it didn't really look like a killer's cabin. Yet, here she was, a lamb being led to the slaughter.

She looked over at her captor. If he stepped out of the car first, she could quickly reverse the car, knocking him down perhaps. However, he looked at her and just waved the gun toward the cabin. Evidently, he had experience abducting people. This didn't bode well for the afternoon. Her pulse raced and her throat suddenly went dry. She opened the door and climbed out.

After she shut the door and started toward the cabin, Doctor Tobias climbed out.

"It's open," he shouted. "Go on in and make yourself comfortable, but leave the car keys on the porch."

Cheryl hoped he was just this thorough because

he was super intelligent and not because he had a lot of experience at abduction and murder. When she walked into the cabin, she was relieved to see it was furnished normally. But then, would a serial killer furnish any differently? She never studied the exceedingly murderous, so she had no way of knowing.

She picked a wooden chair that was a little low to the ground with a large plaid cushion. The fall colors complemented the dark wood nicely. If she wasn't in mortal danger, she might've complimented the doctor on his design choices.

"Won't be long now," Doctor Tobias said as he walked in.

"How do you figure that?" Cheryl asked.

"He spent an entire night with you," Doctor Tobias said as he set the gun on the coffee table just out of Cheryl's reach. "He can track your scent. Your smell has changed, emitting a danger pheromone, if you will. He'll sense you're in danger."

"Great. Now I'm an insect."

Doctor Tobias looked out the windows then turned to Cheryl.

"Tell me you'll kill him while he's killing me."

"Why would he do that? You're mad, completely insane," Cheryl replied. She eyed the gun. They were both about the same distance from it now.

"Anthropology is the study of humanity. I never thought I'd be trying to save it. But, I don't want my death to be in vain," he said. "Promise me!"

Before Cheryl could open her mouth to reply, the window behind Doctor Tobias erupted and a hulking beast landed behind the angry scientist. The creature was covered in dark fur, stood up like a man, but had hairy feet and hands sporting razor sharp claws. It opened its great maw and roared, revealing at least two dozen teeth as long as daggers.

It ripped Doctor Tobias's chest open as the hapless anthropologist turned around. Blood sprayed the room, some of it splashing on Cheryl's face. She gasped, jumped up and grabbed the gun.

The beast saw her and immediately dropped his prey to the ground. Somehow, the doctor still cling to life, moaning and gurgling as blood bubbled from the gaping wound, pooling around him.

Cheryl raised the gun and pointed it at the beast even as the monster transformed before her eyes into her lover.

"My mate," Erich said in a low rumble.

Cheryl's arm trembled. She could feel them together as one now that he was here again in the room. She glanced over at Doctor Tobias, his legs askew and inert; his intestines hung out like glistening worms. She swiveled her arm down and put a bullet in the good doctor's head.

It was the only mercy she could manage.

Erich walked to her and embraced her. Covered in Doctor Tobias's blood, they consummated their love there on the floor, on the kitchen table and finally in the bedroom. It was as savage and primal as before, but this time Cheryl felt more in control and aware even if she gave in to animal lust.

When night arrived, she awoke with Erich still next to her. They were covered in sweat and blood. She never felt more connected to anyone than she did right then. She ran her fingers through Eric's chest hair, watching as his chest rose and fell with his strong even breaths.

He awoke and looked at her.

"How can you melt me with just a glance?" she asked.

"My mother told me it was nature. Our kind connects on a level mere humans can only dream of," Erich said, his deep rumble causing her heart to skip a beat.

"Our kind?"

"Your mother never told you..." Erich said as he touched her face gently.

"She died in a car accident when I was two."

Erich nodded sadly.

"I'm sorry. Siblings?"

"One sister and a brother, but he left home—"

"Before he finished high school," Erich finished. "With no mother, your father…"

"I don't know."

"I'm sorry. You must be so confused. I should have explained before… well, we can catch up another day. We need to jump in the shower. Clean up crew will be here soon."

Erich touched the dried blood on her forearm and it flaked off onto the covers.

"This isn't my first rodeo," he said.

They got off the bed and he held her in his arms again.

"You're so beautiful and strong," he said. "Our children will grow to rule well."

She snuggled her head into his chest and breathed in his scent. She held him tight.

She swore she'd be the best damn brood mother he'd ever known.

# THE CHOICE

**C**ome along, Darren," Charles said as he poured another two fingers of 50-year-old scotch in the crystal goblet. He walked back from the small bar in the expansive living room and sat down in the easy chair across from the couch where Darren Scranton sat glancing around the room at the dozen or so armed figures. "It's a simple transaction."

Darren couldn't figure out the commonality between the armed figures. They seemed to be of multiple nationalities. He looked for a pattern, but outside of being armed and generally dangerous looking, he could find none. Finally, he returned his attention to the lone figure in his easy chair sipping his very expensive scotch like it was water. He glared at the man before a shout from his wife drew his attention to the 78" television they sported in the huge living room. She stood there with their three children cowering behind her. Another half dozen men with weapons casually trained on the remainder of his family were visible, all wearing masks unlike the men in Darren's home. He glared back at Charles.

"I won't pay a ransom. You'll just kill them anyway."

"Would it change your answer if you knew your actions were being recorded and will be broadcast to the world in eight hours?"

For the first time since getting the bum rush from the front door into his living room thirty minutes ago, Darren went pale. Charles smiled as he saw fear and then calculation play out on Darren's face. Among the armed men, three stood filming Darren, careful to keep the others out of frame including the only man who'd spoken since the home invasion began.

"I mean, you can replace a family, right Darren? But how would that look to the public? The adoring fans who've cheered your every success without knowing the true depravity of your machinations. Money? Well, that's another thing easily replaced if you cut the right deals, cut the right corners, and cut out the right people. Like the coal deal in Pennsylvania? Or the prison management contracts and negotiations, like in Dover?"

"How do you know about that?" Darren hissed with a venom he hadn't displayed until know. Charles grinned at the exposed psychological wound of his victim.

"Did you know Mister Elkins, may he rest in peace, recorded every board meeting? And I do mean every board meeting—even the ones in Tuscany. Nice birthmark, by the way—is that a goat?" Charles leaned back in his chair and sipped the scotch. He swirled it around in his mouth and relished the feel on his tongue and teeth.

"Well, if you have that, my reputation is already ruined," Darren seethed.

"I'm not here to ruin anyone's reputation, Mister Scranton. I'm just here to make a few simple transactions and then I'll be on my way. Everyone will be free to go. I will have already exacted my payment from you, nothing more could be gained from lingering or even revisiting your domicile. You recall Mister Elkins family was spared?"

"I don't have that much money," Darren said simply.

Charles looked calmly at Darren and sighed.

"Is ten million per family member spared too much? Are you trying to make a bargain with me?"

"I don't have the money!" Darren shouted.

"I have been nice, so far, civil even and you repay my kindness with bald faced lies. So be it," Charles replied. He turned to his accomplices. "Restrain him."

Two additional men appeared from outside the room, neither with weapons on them but they had considerable builds. Darren stood up, but they quickly subdued him, forced him to his knees, put a gag in his mouth and restrained his arms. They forced his face to look at the television.

Charles took a cell phone from within his black leather jacket and pressed a few buttons.

"Boss?" a male voice answered on speakerphone.

"Mister Scranton requires a demonstration of the gravity of his situation. If I recall, Missus Scranton is right handed. Please remove the left pinky finger," Charles said as if ordering a side of ranch at a restaurant.

Darren struggled and screamed through the gag.

"Oh please, Darren. Felicia is a trophy wife at best. She'll be fine minus a finger. Of course, she will know why she lost it."

On the screen, Darren watched in horror as his wife was restrained in front of their now restrained children. A thug pried open her fingers and cut off a pinky with a small set of pruning shears. Blood sprayed briefly from the wound as Felicia screamed in agony. The children cried and screamed as they struggled to get loose.

The thug then reached into his pocket and got out

a small device. Upon manipulating it, a small flame shot out from the top. He applied the torch to the wound and had it cauterized within moments. Felicia passed out.

"Huh. I thought she'd be a little more hardy then that. You really did just pick her for looks, didn't you Darren?" Charles said.

On the screen, the thug carried Felicia back to the children and lay her down on the ground. He reached in his other pocket, got a bottle of water out, opened it and dumped some on her face. She sputtered awake and immediately grabbed her injured hand, screaming again. The thug put the lid on and set the bottle of water next to her.

"Look at that? A little water to fight off the shock. I really do hire the most considerate people," Charles said as he took a deep swig of the scotch and then set the cup down on the side table. He gave a quick nod to the men restraining Darren. They removed the gag and left him there kneeling on the floor.

"You son of a bitch," Darren said and got to his feet and rushed Charles. Charles supported his body on the arms of the chair as he lifted his feet in the air and kicked Darren in the chest with both feet. There was an audible crack as ribs broke and Darren fell to the floor. Charles stood up.

"You lied, Darren! Seychelles? Bermuda?

Switzerland? I know where all your money is hidden. Don't lie to me again."

Charles sat back down. He looked up at his accomplices.

"Get him back on the couch where he's comfortable," Charles said.

The two men who had restrained him earlier picked him up by his arms and deposited him back on the couch roughly. Darren struggled to breathe. Pain came with every movement of his chest.

"I'm dying," he struggled to get out.

"Not yet," Charles said. He reached into a black bag at his side and pulled out a notebook and pen. He tossed them across the room at Charles. They landed next to him on the couch.

"Login and passwords for the four accounts," Charles said. "We'll take care of the transfers."

"Four?" Darren cried out.

"Do you really need another demonstration? I'm sure little Lilly can get by with only one foot," Charles responded dully.

"No, sorry," Darren grumbled. He wrote the information in the notebook.

"Be careful with your writing. I'll remove one of your toes for each mistake on logging in," Charles said and took another sip of scotch.

Darren paused in his writing. He crossed off two of the passwords and rewrote the correct ones underneath. He set the notebook and pen down and lay back, trying to find a comfortable position to breathe in.

"There," Darren said. "It's all there."

Charles gave another nod to his people. One of them came and retrieved the notebook while another setup a laptop on the bar and got started. Charles got up and made himself another scotch.

"This is truly exquisite, Darren. I admire your taste in 50-year old scotch."

"That was for a special celebration," Darren grumbled.

"I can't imagine a more special occasion than the loss of your considerable ill-gotten wealth," Charles replied and raised the glass to toast Darren, who simply rolled his eyes.

Darren groaned in agony for the next forty-five minutes until the man at the laptop gave a thumbs up.

Charles pulled out his cell phone again and checked his own accounts and smiled. He made a few transactions of his own and then nodded to the man at the laptop, who shut the laptop down and walked out of the building. He pressed a few more buttons and got the same thug from earlier on the phone.

"Operation complete, let them go," Charles said.

On the screen the armed thugs moved away from Darren's family. A few moments later, vehicles could be seen pulling away in the distance behind them on a dirt road. The view from the drone camera rose into the air and the signal cut out.

"There we are," Charles replied. "Your family is free to go. They've got a bit of a walk ahead of them as they're ten miles from the nearest road, but I'm sure they'll be fine. Good thing you didn't get Lilly's foot cut off. Can you imagine the hassle of trying to get all the way back with her unable to walk?"

"How do I know you'll keep your word?" Darren replied.

"You don't but I really don't have any reason to harm them now that I have harmed you," Charles replied.

"What are you talking about?"

"You are a high functioning sociopath. You find your value in life from the pain you can inflict, the money and goods you can acquire and the false reputation you've built for yourself. Your respect, as it were, in the community."

"I'll be fine," Darren replied. "I know people. I'll get my money back and I'll find you. You won't live beyond the reach of an assassin's bullet."

"You see, Darren, here's where you miss the entire point of this exercise," Charles said as he sat next to him on the couch. He took out a pocketknife, opened it and stabbed it into Darren's thigh.

Darren screamed out in pain.

Charles removed the knife, wiped the blood off on Darren's pants, folded it back up and slid it back into his pocket. Darren grabbed his wound and pressed into it, trying to stop the bleeding.

"This is the point where you bargain for your own life, and you've really started out badly by threatening mine," Charles said. "What do you think about starting these negotiations again, hmm?"

"You're a maniac!" Darren hollered.

"Well, I have been accused of some things in my lifetime, that's certainly among the more common accusations," Charles said and chuckled. "My wife used to tell me I was crazy and out of my mind, but, at the time, it was all in good fun. Sarcastic fun between a husband and wife."

"I'm going to bleed to death," Darren grunted.

"Well, we'll make sure you get the best of care if you can keep your end of the bargain, of course."

"You've already got all of my money," Darren whimpered.

"You remember that little event in Dover I mentioned earlier?" Charles asked.

"I don't know what you're talking about," Darren

replied.

Charles smacked his hand down on top of Darren's hands holding his wound. Darren screamed out in pain.

"I really thought we'd gotten this lying thing worked out," Charles said. "Now I don't have your family to threaten anymore, so we'll just have to take it out on your body, Darren."

Charles raised his hand and three of his accomplices dragged Darren from the couch and held him down as a fourth removed one of his shoes. Darren hollered the entire time and shouted in agony when the fourth man pulled out the small garden shears and cut off his pinky toe in much the same manner as Felicia had lost her pinky. It was followed by a small hand torch which the man used to cauterize the wound.

The men then got off of Darren and left him groveling on the floor, crying out in pain.

"Now, Darren, do you remember the little event in Dover?" Charles asked loudly from the couch.

"Yes," Darren shouted. "Dammit, you cut off my toe!"

"Oh, I'm very aware of what I've done, Darren. What we're trying to get to the bottom of is what you did," Charles said. "Oh, dear, I've forgotten my scotch."

Charles got up and kicked Darren's head as he

walked by on his way to the easy chair. Darren grabbed his head and shouted out again. Charles sat down in the chair and picked up the glass for a quick sip. He took a deep breath.

"Now, Darren, what happened at Dover?"

"The company recalled all the prison guards to get a better contract," Darren said between gritted teeth. "But it wasn't—"

"Careful, Darren. You only have nine toes left," Charles advised him.

"It wasn't only my decision. The board voted," Darren said.

"Was the new contract for better conditions for the prisoners, rehabilitation or medical or something?" Charles asked, knowing full well the answer.

"No," Darren grumbled.

"Was it for better pay for the guards and personnel, better benefits perhaps?" Charles asked. He took another sip of his scotch as he waited for the answer.

"No," Darren said. He took a deep breath in and then whimpered as the pain in his ribs fought with the pain in his leg and foot for supremacy in his brain.

"How many prison facilities were under your company's management, Darren," Charles asked.

"I'm not sure. A hundred or so," Darren groaned.

"One hundred and twenty-two. I won't count that as a lie, Darren. I will just count it as carelessness or perhaps apathy as to the real extent of your own business holdings. Crass disregard? No, I think that's saved for what happened at Dover. Did any of the other facilities have the personnel in charge of the prison walk off the job?"

"No."

"You know, I really like this scotch. 50 years old. I mean, it's got to be an amazing feat to even have anymore left in the cask after 50 years. It's kind of a magic number for scotch, don't you think?" Charles asked as he got up and refilled his glass.

"I guess so," Darren replied.

"Do you mind if I take it with me when I leave? It's got an unmatchable flavor. Really something to savor," Charles said as he sat back down.

"Sure, why not?" Darren groaned. "You've taken everything else."

"You know, that's kind of how everyone I work with feels about you, Darren."

"What?"

"Why did the board vote to have everyone at the Dover facility walk off the job?" Charles asked.

"To send a message to the government," Darren replied.

"Oh, I think they heard it," Charles said. "What they didn't hear was a warning from your management that you would be having this little walk off. Did they, Darren?"

Darren grimaced but said nothing.

"They were sent an email," Darren replied.

"At 5pm as the personnel were walking off the job, correct?"

"A contractual oversight," Darren replied. "The company was fined."

"The company was fined." Charles nodded. "Fifty-seven prisoners escaped that night from an unmanned facility fourteen hours before someone noticed an email from your company."

"What's your point?" Darren grumbled.

"Your company wanted an increase of five hundred thousand dollars per facility under your management. Sixty-one million dollars of pure profit annually. To accomplish this profit, you and your board decided it was worth letting prisoners escape to force the government's hand," Charles said as he set down the glass.

"It's just business," Darren said. "Nothing personal."

"That's what I think, too, Darren!" Charles exclaimed. "Everyone here agrees. Everyone here who had family members living in the Dover area who were slaughtered by those escaped prisoners that night agrees. They all agree our visit here, to your house, is just business. The business of recompense. The business of justice. The business of revenge. The business of dues owed and dues paid."

"I can't undo the past," Darren grumbled.

"No," Charles said. "But we can make sure you never repeat it. I've had my single stab at your pathetic miserable existence. One little wound in your thigh to recompense me for the loss of my wife, two daughters and son to a convicted rapist and murderer who visited my family that night. Now, Mister Scranton, the others shall have their due."

Each of Charles' accomplices came to Darren and stabbed him, some of them repeatedly. At first Darren cried out for mercy, plead for forgiveness and finally fell silent as the wounds overtook him. The pool of blood grew around him as he bled out.

As Charles walked out, he grabbed the bottle of 50-year-old scotch and lit the accelerant that had been spread throughout the building. He wasn't certain Darren was dead yet, but he was certain that would no longer be a question after the fire consumed his home and his body.

9 781590 928691